DREAM

Also by Kate Grenville

Bearded Ladies
Lilian's Story

KATE GRENVILLE

DREAMHOUSE

University of Queensland Press

First published 1986 by University of Queensland Press
Box 42, St Lucia, Queensland, Australia
Reprinted in paperback 1987

Typeset and printed in Australia by The Book Printer, Melbourne

Cataloguing in Publication Data

National Library of Australia

Grenville, Kate, 1950–
  Dreamhouse.

  I. Title.

A823'.3

ISBN 0 7022 2053 1

The author is grateful to Simone Alcorso for her help with the Italian, and is pleased to acknowledge the assistance of the International Association of University Women (US) in the completion of this book.

1

My husband was a vain man with a thick orange moustache who loved to look at his beautiful wife, slim like a model and striking on the streets. *Look,* people nudged each other. *Look at her!* He liked to see them nudge each other, and liked to watch me across tables or from the far side of a room, pleased with his thick orange moustache and his striking wife. As for myself, I was a woman full of greed: my husband, whose name was Reynold, was soon to be a professor with an income and a position, while I could never be anything wealthier than a striking secretary with lovely legs and little future.

We drove towards our summer in Tuscany, taking wrong turnings in three countries and asking directions of wooden-faced locals who gestured vaguely down the road. We had been looking forward to our summer in Italy, although I had wondered if Rennie's vanity and my greed would survive a foreign summer, alone with each other for so long. Here there would be no parties or streets where we could glitter. Rennie had joked about it: *Think you'll be putting cyanide in my tea by August, darling?* as if he was not sure either, behind his powerful moustache.

We kept asking for Aretta, as Daniel had told us to. But all those leathery farmers, and their wives with aprons full of beans, shook their heads blankly. At last Rennie lost patience with peasants who refused to understand his version of Italian, and drove fast along the narrow lanes, turning right and left at random, thrusting his chin out in the way he did when life was misbehaving. Finally, at the top of a hill we saw the same view of Florence below for the third time, and he agreed to stop and let me try asking the way.

I used my fingers to mark the pages of useful phrases in *Italian for Fun,* still crisp and untried. I was made reckless by all this tiresome driving and chin-thrusting.

— *Per favore,* I read slowly, *Per favore, Signora, dov'è Aretta?*

It was a woman in black with heavy stockings that had fallen around her ankles, and she was dangling a hen from one hand and a cleaver from the other. She shook her head and muttered and gestured up and down the road with the flapping hen, saying something that was not in the book. She did not seem to be saying *To the left, to the right,* or *straight on.* Rennie stared in front of him and tapped his fingers on the wheel but I was desperate enough to try another of the names Daniel had written down for us. When she heard it, the woman's face split into a smile that showed a single tooth and the cleaver glittered as it pointed up the road.

— *San Giorgio, sì, sì, a sinistra, sempre sinistra.*

— *Grazie,* I read, then said, but Rennie accelerated away up the road, whipping my head back and leaving the woman and her doomed hen behind in the floating dust.

We sped *a sinistra* along the lanes then, through tiny villages with long pious names, where all the shutters on the faded walls were closed against the sun. Were they all ghost towns? Or were sleepy villagers, woken from their naps by the car, coming to the windows in their vests to squint at the bright streets, and the car with the steering-wheel on the wrong side?

Across the side of a barren slope of olive trees, we were forced to grind along behind a tractor with a bright green umbrella attached to the back that swayed with every

2

rubbery bounce of the machine. The driver's face under the umbrella was a luminous green and even his teeth were asparagus-colour as he turned to grin and wave at us with flamboyant ambiguous gestures. Locked behind him, sweating in the cramped car, we were getting tired of smiling and waving back. Rennie finally took the risk of becoming another statistic, and overtook the grinning green farmer on yet another blind corner.

Daniel had said, *Look for the flags, you can't miss them.* But we missed them until Rennie finally spotted the bare flagpole above the trees. As we slowed down to drive up the rutted track that led to the house, the car became intolerable, now that the journey was nearly over: cramped, noisy, and full of insufferably hot air.

Daniel was a professor in London, a professor with beautiful suits and small feet. *Your husband will matter,* he told me. *Rennie will matter one day, but first he must finish the dissertation.* Daniel owned land as well as suits, a property in Tuscany where he had lived with his wife, an Italian signora of means. His two children, his son and daughter, still lived on this property, in one of the two villas. *A villa:* I heard that word and became languorous, with visions of balustrades, a view of blue water, cool white wine, bare feet on marble. *My villa,* Daniel said, *spend the summer there, dear boy, and get that wretched dissertation done.*

So we were to arrive at the first villa, where the children lived, and they would direct us to the second villa, where we would spend our summer.

At the house with the flagpole, we rang the doorbell again and again but finally, reluctantly, had to recognize that Hugo and Viola were not at home. We stood wondering what to do, and covered our ears against the outraged barking of a dog that threatened us with long yellow teeth, tugging at the chain that held it within inches

3

of the wall of the house. Its bark seemed piercing enough to bring crowds storming out of the woods to drive off the strangers. As we stared up at the windows of the villa, we did our best to look like friends of the family. The dog knew, though, and we knew. We knew we were foreigners, and did not speak the language.

Looking for another door at the back of the house, we found two small wild birds tethered to the ground by lengths of fishing line. The birds leapt and leapt into the air, but each time their twig-like legs were nearly pulled out of their sockets and they fell back to the ground. They had worn a circular bald patch in the grass, but they fluttered in silence.

Through the glass of the back door we could see the empty kitchen, which had the smug tidiness of a decoy. One wall of the room was covered with identical clocks, like the ones in railway stations, and each one showed a different time. Rennie peered in, then pushed back his cuff to glance at his watch, and I listened at the glass. I held my breath, but my ears were still humming after the hours in the car. I could not tell if the whirring I could hear was from the clocks or from the tired machinery in my own head.

—Wonder how long they'll be.

Rennie had taken off his watch to wind it, but he almost dropped it, jumping backwards in fright as one of the birds blundered against his leg. I looked away as he wiped with a leaf at the runny white gob on his shoe, and would have liked to have jumped back into that intolerable car and driven away. That did not seem possible, and I sat down on the steps with Rennie to wait for Daniel's children.

The afternoon sun had left the steps now, and the shadow of the house was reaching over the vineyards that sloped down the hill. Over the snarling and barking of the dog, we discussed the possibility that the house on the opposite ridge might be the one we were going to stay in. We were polite to each other, and did not say *No,* always *Yes, but* . . . A habit of surface had grown between us and in spite of dogs and horrors, we were bland and conversed well. Rennie pointed out that there was a house on top of almost every ridge, wherever we looked. He was so persuasive, and the landscape revealed so many earth-coloured, crumbling houses when looked at closely, that we almost convinced each other that this was the wrong house altogether, in spite of the flagpole.

At last a dull grey van like a riot-truck bumped up the track. We stood uncertainly. This could be the happy ending, the arrival of our hosts to let us begin our summer in Tuscany. Or it could be the story of misunderstanding with Italian police. If we looked like trespassers or thieves, how would we explain that we were not what we seemed to be?

The windscreen reflected the sky so that whoever was inside the van was invisible, but when the door opened the two people who stepped out were obviously Daniel's children. Even for brother and sister they looked very alike. Their silence was like the silence of one person, their poise like a piece of china on a quiet mantelpiece. They were young, but they moved like a couple used to being stared at admiringly, and their smooth faces looked as if they would never become ugly with emotion. Rennie advanced on them with a confident outstretched hand.

— Hello, I'm Rennie Dufrey and this is my wife Louise. Did Daniel tell you to expect us?

The two bland faces seemed prepared to deflect any amount of bonhomie. Hugo smiled as he shook hands but his nod looked more like resignation than an answer.

— Yes, we were expecting you.

From his boarding-school English no one would have

guessed that his mother was Italian. Viola stared at me and said nothing so I thought perhaps she did not speak English. There was a silence in which all four of us stood looking at each other, a silence in which Rennie's smile went flaccid. Viola finally spoke, over-solicitous like any reluctant hostess, and in perfect English:

— I expect you'd like to go straight to the other house.

Nothing in the manner of this couple urged us to stay, and something about the long wait, the tortured dog, the tortured birds, made the words pop out of my mouth:

— Yes, yes please.

The brother and sister started to say something at once, and exchanged a glance. Then Hugo said:

— Just keep going up the road. It's that house over there. You have the key, don't you?

Rennie held it up and joked about how it was like a dungeon key. He spoke rather loudly to make it clear he was joking. Viola and Hugo stared at him patiently. They did not seem to expect fun or boredom from their visitors, these friends of their father's, but were just determined to endure us. Rennie had lost faith in his little joke by the time Hugo finally spoke.

— Domenico will bring you bread every day. There is no need to pay him.

Rennie began to protest vaguely but Viola was already moving towards the house and interrupted him to speak over her shoulder.

— You must ask if you need anything.

Hugo moved away to a shed beside the house. It seemed unnecessary and even inappropriate to keep on thanking or greeting or farewelling, but when Rennie started the engine its noise filled the silence rudely. As the hot little car bounced over the ruts I glanced back and saw Hugo come out of the shed holding a scrap of bright cloth.

— Perhaps they're shy, Rennie said. Perhaps they'll improve on acquaintance.

My husband, that man of optimism, did not look at me as he spoke, so he did not have to see me shake my head.

— Don't you think? he asked after a moment, and looked at me, but I had finished shaking my head.

— Don't you think? he asked again.

I did not, but I did not say so.

He refused to be discouraged when the key would not budge in the rusted lock of the front door, and set off to look for a small window with Boy Scout resourcefulness and cheer. I picked my way through the blackberries after him, trying not to think about spiders and snakes, and feeling spied on. I wished I had asked Viola for a cup of tea. Rennie enjoyed smashing the smallest window with the heel of his shoe and I felt he regretted being too large for the hole.

— Careful, Louise, he kept saying as I took hold of the rotten frame to pull myself up. Careful now.

As I pulled myself through, I felt my palm slide across an edge of glass and cobwebs brush my face. For a moment I was stuck halfway and had to fight panic.

— You okay? I heard Rennie call from behind me, but he was in the world I was leaving. I was entering a foreign one that smelled of mould and was dark, the unknown interior of a strange house.

— You okay, Louise?

My toes finally struck the floor and I let myself down into a small damp room, crouching, expecting a blow, feeling the blood sticky between my fingers.

7

2

Daniel had described the house as rustic and had apologized for offering it to us for the summer. *It's terribly primitive dear boy,* he had said, and smoothed a lapel of his beautiful suit. *I am ashamed dear boy.* We'd expected a lot of turned and varnished wood, bunches of dried flowers everywhere, and perhaps even an old well in the middle of a garden overgrown with roses. We hadn't imagined that Daniel's description was a euphemism for the last stages of decay.

When we began exploring the house we tiptoed and whispered to each other like trespassers. *What? Find something?* Rennie thought I spoke when I said nothing, and thought I found something—what was he looking for?—when there was nothing to find. Every room we went into was dark and silent. When the shutters were pushed back against the clenched hinges, yellow Tuscan light filled the air, but revealed nothing more sinister than a scattering of mouse-droppings. Under the rotten ceiling of the middle room upstairs, there was a heap of acid-white bird-dropping from the murmurous dove-loft in the roof, and birds peered down at us through the hole in the ceiling, ruffling their wings and shifting uneasily.

Next door in the corner room, the shutters yielded to a push and fell away into the bushes outside. The window-frame sagged suddenly inwards and we stepped back. Rennie looked up at the beams above us that supported the roof. They did not collapse as we watched, but we could see deep cracks running the length of each one. The adze marks of two centuries before could still be seen on the dry wood, so that I imagined the hot sweat running off the backs of men labouring to build this house: *It will stand forever,* they would have told each other, and slapped each beam, still bleeding sap, and they would have gone to their wives at night and held them all the more fervently for thinking they were building something that would last forever. A colossal weight of terracotta tiles bore down on the beams that those men had shaped, weight bearing down year after year and teasing the brittle grain of the wood further and further apart, towards the final collapse that would send clouds of dust and astonished doves into the air. But those adze-men would not have thought about that.

Along the hall, in a big room with a view, Rennie stamped on the floor to see if it would hold, glanced up at the ceiling where only a few flakes of plaster drifted down, and decided that this was the best room to work in. There was a table in the room and he dragged it over to the window for a desk.

—All set for the summer darling, he said, and I felt fear at the idea of this particular stretch of my future, not wanting to think as far ahead as a whole summer.

There were three narrow beds in this room, each with a cover of clear plastic over the mattress. In one of them a family of mice had made a nest in the mattress among the kapok and the springs. It was a cosy home, but exposed like a display under the plastic. Four baby mice, like thick pink maggots, wormed slowly over each other in the centre of the nest while the bigger mice nosed further into the wadding between the springs, enlarging the nest. This happy family seemed to think it was invisible, safe under its plastic, and was not disturbed by the people bending over it.

—Think someone's watching us like this?

Rennie poked at the plastic over the nest and the mice stopped shifting around each other. They listened, felt the air with their whiskers twitching, perhaps prayed.

—I feel like God, Rennie said.

I fancied the idea of being God, too, and pressed up and down on the mattress so that the nest bounced and the mice scrabbled and clawed over each other's backs. One of them slipped up out of the nest and slid along between the plastic and the mattress, towards the edge of the bed. Escape! A worthy dream. But like any god I had my cruel streak, and was not ready for escape just yet. I pressed down on the bed and tightened the cover on either side of this bold escaping mouse until its fur flattened and its tiny head struggled against the plastic squeezing down on it. It was a despicable triumph, but it was a triumph, and when the mouse gave up the struggle and lay as if dead I released it. Like any other chastened explorer it turned and crept back the way it had come, back into the nest.

—Great view darling. Better than that foul orange fence at home.

I came to stand beside him at the window to agree about the great view. The badly-shaved cheek of a patchy field of wheat curved down to a wooded valley and a matching field curved up the other side of the house on the opposite hill, where small wild birds were slowly killing themselves in despair. It seemed possible to walk out of this window across the air into the same window across the valley, where the limp flag of a curtain shifted along the wall from time to time. Watching in silence, we waited to see Hugo and Viola appear but they did not, and Rennie turned away from the window. He brushed a grey line of cobweb off the front of my shirt and said:

—We'll be able to afford a view when we go back to London. No more orange fences.

He kicked at a sheet of newspaper beside the table, revealing a small hole in the wall at floor-level and a scattering of mortar.

— Ah. The mice.

He bent down and pushed a finger in, but pulled it out again quickly. I watched the back of his head and wondered if he was remembering warnings from childhood about how dangerous fingers in holes could be.

— Like mascots, coming and going while I work.

He pulled the paper back loosely over the hole and stood looking at it and smiling. When my husband smiled, his orange moustache became twisted and alive under his nose. There were times when I would have liked to rip it off his face.

— As long as they don't take a fancy to the inside of my pants-leg, of course.

We laughed together at that good joke, because it was only Louise, the lovely wife of Reynold, who was supposed to take a fancy to the inside of her husband's pants-leg.

Long Italian dusk was darkening from moment to moment now, and our first night in our villa was about to begin. We decided to use only two of the upstairs rooms, and left the others, full of the smell of mould and mouse-droppings, to breathe and crumble quietly behind closed doors. In the back room with the murkily mirrored wardrobe, we swept up the mouse-dirt and made the bed.

We ate a dry meal of leftover sandwiches in the kitchen and could hear the mice beginning to play through the house, and plopping and squeaking scratchily. Going upstairs in the dark I heard Rennie's heavy boots ahead of me on the stairs and waited for the squelch.

We climbed into the high bed and lay stiffly, feeling the strangeness of the house, or of each other.

— Goodnight darling, Rennie said.

11

—Goodnight darling, I said back.

He began breathing heavily beside me and the bedclothes stirred regularly over his rounded back. He was a tidy sleeper, so it was hard to be certain when he was really asleep. If I whispered *Fire!* would he bounce up, fling the bedclothes back, leap to the window? The bed was almost too narrow for a couple, but even so my husband made a space between our bodies. When I slid across to curve myself against his back, he retreated further, to the very edge of the bed. He seemed prepared to fall out of this high bed rather than feel me curved around him. I did not want to have him fall out of our bed, so I slid back to my own side. I listened to the pattering and scratching of the mice through the house, and thought about grossly obese women and their reinforced mattresses. I had heard that the tiny husbands of such women were forced to slide to the floor, pad around the bed, and get in on the other side, when their wife felt the urge to turn over in bed. I would not enjoy being such a husband, in danger of suffocation. I would not enjoy being such a wife, either, trapped by fat. In the connubial bed of our London flat, Rennie had liked plenty of space between our bodies, but there, in a bigger bed, it had been less obvious.

Before we could make the bed in this room, we had had to shake a layer of grit off the cover and pillows. Throughout every day and every night, tiny flakes of plaster had come loose from the ceiling and floated down, with grains of sawdust that trickled out of the thousands of pin-point holes that riddled the beams above the bed. Those beams! They looked so strong, so massively rough-hewn, and they were as weak as grass. The light rain of debris would go on falling as we lay under it, and I lay feeling or imagining it falling on my face and on Rennie's breathing back. How long would it take, lying still, to be smothered completely? Perhaps before that could happen, the whole house would fold in on itself. I thought about the lingering way buildings fall to their knees when subjected to the wrong kind of stress.

The scrabble of claws over tiles carried through the still house like the silly scratch of a watch held to the ear. I fingered myself between my legs and when I closed my eyes I imagined the twitching noses of inquisitive mice, their eyes alert and unblinking in the darkness as they took stock of the intruders. The back of my hand rasped against the sheet, and I heard my breath coming more quickly, until my knees fell away from each other and I was consumed by white pleasure like a bonfire. Back in London I'd known just how to set the bed squeaking and make such a friction in the space between our bodies that I could no longer believe Rennie was asleep. But asleep or not, he seldom turned to me full of lust and the dream of pleasure. He lay on, breathing blamelessly or guiltily, not touching his wife as she writhed beside him. I listened to his steady breathing and wondered if his eyes were wide open on the dark, staring at the grey square of the window, concentrating on keeping his breathing as unhurried as someone lost in peaceful dreams.

I envied the simplicity of his deceit. Mine would have to be more elaborate. I jammed my forefinger up into myself as far as it would go, then held it up to my face, straining to see in the dark, sniffing, finally licking at it tentatively with the tip of my tongue. There was still no sign, no stickiness, no sharp metallic taste. How much longer would Rennie not notice the gap in the rhythm of my months? How much longer did I have, before he would guess at the possibility of a new being embedded in my flesh, swelling on my blood? How sweetly he'd kiss me — *That's wonderful darling* — and what a hug he'd give me. How easy it was to imagine the bewilderment — *but of course we want to keep it!* His eyes would watch me then, watch my every move, and I would never be able to escape.

3

In the morning a dead mouse lay curled by the door and the loose wallpaper in the next room flapped like someone preparing to speak and thinking better of it.

—Morning, darling, Rennie said, propped up on his elbow in the bed, the brown nightshirt hiked up around his waist. With his forefinger he traced a crease like a scar on his shoulder.

—I love you, darling, he said, and dragged the nightshirt down.

—I love you too, I said, feeling my lips shape themselves stiffly around the words. I stared into Rennie's eyes and tried it backwards to myself: *Uoy evoli.*

—You look a hundred miles away, he said. Had a dream or something?

I shook my head and wondered what he would say if I told him I was imagining how this roof could cave in and the beams crush him like a cockroach.

—I was wondering what that hook was for, I said, and he finally looked away from me at the ceiling.

—Hanging hares or hams or something. Or maybe Daniel hanged his wife.

When I laughed the bed squeaked as its old joints moved against each other and under cover of laughing I slid over to Rennie's side, feeling my bare thigh against his and reaching a hand down under the bedclothes. My lips touched his at the same moment that my fingers brushed into his groin and he arched away from both points of contact like a hooked fish. He rubbed his lips hard as if stung, then laughed.

15

—That tickled.

He gave me a fleeting dry kiss on the neck before turning away and throwing back the covers as if letting light into a dark room. Once safely out of bed, the heavy nightshirt falling as far as his ankles, he bent down to kiss my mouth, but when I tried to pull him closer, he straightened up out of the embrace. His smile as he pulled on his shorts and running shoes was one of satisfaction. I pulled my nightgown up to my armpits and ran my hands down my body.

—Too much good living darling? Am I getting fat and ugly?

With one foot up on a box tying a lace he looked at me.

—I can still count your ribs.

He pushed at my body until I had rolled over onto my stomach, and one hand cupped each buttock as he said:

—You know I like something to hang on to.

I did know that, and could still feel the bruises from the last time he had rolled me over onto my stomach and thrust into me, violently and briefly, crushing my flesh under his hands. It did not happen often, and it was not much fun. Each time, I wondered who it was he was thrusting into, behind his tightly-squeezed closed eyes. But today was not one of those days. He gave my buttocks a final painful squeeze and turned away, putting on the clothes for the morning run that he never missed.

With one side of my face hidden in the pillow I lay and watched as he carefully lined up the right buttons with the right holes in his shirt, and when he had finished I dragged the sheet up from my feet and over my head. He combed his hair before turning to the bed, and squeezed my toe through the sheet.

—See you later darling.

His rubber soles squeaked down the stairs and across the living room and the hens set up a panicked flapping and clucking when he disturbed them outside the front door. I flung the sheet back and thrust my fingers up into myself one more time, but there was still no sign. I told myself it was just that I was worrying too much, that it would be all right if I could forget about it.

Before getting out of bed I took my nightgown off and threw it down on the floor, listening for mice. As I brushed my hair in front of the wardrobe I avoided my eyes in the mirrored door and had a fright when my face slid sideways as the door swung open, slyly revealing the clothes hanging inside and a scattering of mouse-droppings beside my galoshes. I checked the pockets of my skirt for mice before putting it on and went downstairs feeling last night's droppings crush beneath my sandals.

The kitchen was like a room from a different house. It was the only room that had been finished when the renovation had been abandoned, and while the rest of the house was on the point of collapse, this room gleamed with stainless steel and white tiles. In the rest of the house there was barely enough furniture for even basic needs, but this room was prepared for any kind of operation, with spatulas, graters, whisks like the diagram of an atom, blenders, mixers, dicers. In each drawer the knives lay smugly in their trays — smiling curved ones for grapefruit, heavy ones for steak, fish knives with a nick in each blade like a shark's mouth. The only decorations in the room were more knives: rows of steel choppers and slicers, knives for paring, knives for peeling, knives for coring, knives for opening oysters. At the end of the row, the massive square cleaver hung ready for use at a moment's notice. I had never before used a kitchen with even one sharp knife. Now I thought of the tough stewing meat I would buy in order to use the heavy choppers, imagined the pleasure I would take in shattering chicken carcasses with the blunt-nosed cleaver, and planned to buy oysters if I could.

I had my back to the door, putting water on to boil, when I felt the room darken, and almost screamed when I saw the figure blocking the light in the doorway was not Rennie. I backed up against the stove, feeling the warmth of its flame dangerous against my back, and the man in the doorway advanced on me. It was only when he was close to me, and I had given up the idea of throwing the panful of water at him, that I saw he was old, toothless, bent. He was saying something, shouting more loudly as I continued not to understand, and was starting to jab at my chest with a finger so I was fighting panic when I realized he was not shouting abuse or accusation.

—*Buon giorno,* he was shouting, and I could remember that much from the phrase book.

—*Buon giorno,* I cried back, so that the kitchen rang with sound. *Buon giorno.*

We had come to the end of the pleasure of repeating *Buon giorno* at each other, and nodding and smiling, when this old man began to jab himself in the chest and shout *Domenico,* separating each syllable so it was like a chant.

—Louise, I yelled back and saw his face split apart with the joy of communication.

— Ah! Louisa! he cried, and I did not mind being Louisa for Domenico.

Like a magician bringing a snake out of a hat, Domenico suddenly produced a loaf of bread from behind his back and thrust it at me.

—*Pane,* he yelled so that spittle landed on my face.

I nodded and repeated it: *Pane,* and Domenico slapped my shoulder with a hard countryman's hand and laughed a terrible toothless cackle at the foreigner who had just

18

learned to say *bread,* backed up against someone else's stove and grinning stiffly.

He turned to go but remembered something and with elaborate hand-over-hand gestures shouted some more words at me, the furrow between his eyebrows deepening as I continued to be obtuse.

—*Domani,* he shouted, and I could repeat it but could not guess what it meant: his other name? The kind of bread? A question? A warning? Finally he shrugged and made a leave-taking gesture with a flat palm, as if he was polishing a pane of glass between us, and left. A flurry of hens ran after him for their breakfast as he walked back across the yard to his barn.

I picked out a grapefruit from the basket, feeling saliva gush into my mouth at the thought of the tart juice. From the drawer full of knives I chose one exactly suited to the job. I had seen grapefruit knives before, but never had the pleasure of using a left-handed one. I relished the way the two halves fell away from the blade and the way the sharp serrations sliced the pith from the fruit.

—Darling it's a wonderful day. And I saw a humming-bird.

Rennie stood blinking in the sun at the doorway, glowing from his mile-and-a-half. When I turned to him our smiles slid off each other and his face was featureless against the brightness outside.

—Wonderful, I said. How wonderful.

The sharp blade continued to split off each segment of fruit from the next with dreadful smoothness and I heard the words steaming effortlessly off the top of my thoughts.

—Was that the chap with the bread, the old fellow I saw?

Rennie picked up the loaf and tossed it from hand to hand as if it was still hot.

— Do you think they meant it, about not paying him?

He bent and stretched in the doorway, touching his toes and straightening again. I could imagine him lined up with the other boys in some huge green gym, panting, guffawing, wrestling later, falling against the lockers.

— Better ask Hugo, I said, cutting the grapefruit into smaller and smaller segments for the pleasure of the way the blade sliced through the fruit.

He straightened up one last time and stood feet apart, jerking his elbows back at chest height, hands level under his chin. *I must, I must, increase my bust,* I used to snicker with the other girls, all in our bottle-green bloomers, thrusting our elbows back and giggling. Those days seemed in an impossibly distant past, before I had become a lovely woman, and a wife. In the ecstasy of the final ritual, Rennie closed his eyes and rolled his head around on his shoulders, circling his face back and around with swooning abandon. In pregnancy, nipples turned brown, breasts engorged, and the whole pelvis spread so that a shiny head could force its way out into the light, covered with blood, bawling.

We sat on opposite sides of the huge marble table that almost filled the kitchen. I laid a cloth in front of each chair because the chill of the marble was numbing our wrists. As we ate, I found my fingertips exploring the edge of the table. It was so much like a cadaver-slab I was looking for the gutter grooved around the edge for the blood.

Rennie's face puckered at the first mouthful of fruit, and he gobbled quickly to get it down. I stared at the white marble and ate steadily, thinking about sweet things: honey and chocolate and the dripping pulp of an over-ripe mango. I laid my spoon down with a sigh when the last shreds were gone.

— What's up darling? Why the big sigh?

20

I shook my head, and made my face smile, staring at Rennie but picturing a chill shuttered room with a tiled floor, and myself standing in front of the desk before some dome-headed doctor, stumbling in Italian and finally, obscenely, gesturing what I meant. I would have to bend my knees and point them outwards like a Charleston and make pulling gestures with my hands. It was possible he could have me arrested.

— Well darling, up to the salt mines.

Rennie wiped his mouth and smoothed his moustache caressingly. I continued to sit staring at the scooped pith shells, listening to his heavy feet going up the stairs and along the passage, first to the bathroom to shower away the sweat of his run, then to the embyro room, where his chair scraped along the floor as he sat at the desk and got out his notes on *Malthus and the Doctrine of Necessary Catastrophe*. I heard the clink of the mineral water bottle against the glass and could imagine him taking a mouthful and throwing his head back to gargle briefly and loudly before spitting out the window, burping, and uncapping the fountain-pen.

Standing at the sink washing the breakfast plates, I could not see the whole of the house on the other hill, as Rennie could from his desk above me. But the upper storey was visible above the trees, and the flagpole Daniel had told us about, with a small flag fluttering today, like the ones that meant *In Quarantine* or *Plague Aboard,* that I knew ships flew when they came into port. Perhaps they meant something else for Daniel's children, or perhaps they meant nothing at all. I remembered the scrap of bright cloth in Hugo's hand, though, and did not think they meant nothing. For those like me, who did not understand their language, the flags were at least a bright spot in this repetitious landscape. Every olive grove here clawed into the sky like the next one, and at the top of

21

every hill the same brown house stood, secretly crumbling
a little more with each day that passed.

4

The barn where Domenico lived in darkness with the animals was a squat stone structure that would probably outlast the house by a couple of centuries. His voice emerged muffled from the fortress-thick walls, but when he paced backwards and forwards near the doorway and yelled at an imagined or invisible audience, his voice carried clearly across the yard to the house. The animals were not alarmed by his shouting, and seemed to dance to his harangues. He shouted in rage, and the doves swooped down from the loft, their slow wings making a noise like unoiled hinges, and settled along the top of a crumbling stone arch. His voice became musical, a chant that could have been *sì, per favore, sì, per favore, sì, sì,* and the doves all spread their wings at once and dropped down to the wheat field. *Prego, prego, prego,* he shrieked on a rising inflection like despair, and a line of hens ran quickly out of the barn and into the wheat. Dull wooden sounds like light furniture being shifted carried faintly across the yard.

I listened each afternoon, sitting up at the window with the typewriter and Rennie's notes in front of me. In person, Domenico was always smiling, and never spoke more than a word or two at a time. This voice of his harangues he kept for his other life, invisible in the barn. I stopped typing and strained to listen, but even when a phrase or two carried clearly across the yard, the words did not seem to be any of the ones I had learned from the phrase-book. Finally I returned to my typing, taking Domenico's rage for granted as the hens did.

Furniture was sparse in this house, and we'd found that the table Rennie used in the embryo room was the only kind of desk. Each afternoon when I started work I had to make sure that my chair was standing securely on the middle of the coffee table before I climbed up carefully and pulled the typewriter towards me on top of the tall chest of drawers where I worked. Beside the typewriter was a carbon copy of another chapter of *Malthus and the Doctrine of Necessary Catastrophe,* ready to be mailed back to London for safety, in case some act of God took place in Tuscany. It appalled me, the number of fires or floods that would have to take place all over Europe for the whole thing to be lost.

Typing from Rennie's notes was slow work, and I have always hated typing. Even as a lovely secretary I had hated it, but Rennie had promised this would be the only time he would ask me. *For the next book we'll be rich, darling,* he had promised. So I sat each afternoon on my precarious seat and typed. In the quiet house, the din of the typewriter seemed very loud in spite of the folded towel Rennie had suggested I put under the machine. *It just echoes right up the stairs darling.* I did not try to explain that I had enjoyed the angry clatter.

Because of Rennie's scribbles and corrections, I had to hesitate often at a word in his notes, and mouth possibilities like someone prompting a ouija board, so it was impossible not to read the words I was typing and absorb their meaning. That could have been why I made so many mistakes, although, having lovely legs, I had never needed to be a very good typist. It could have been why I typed *Maltux* or *Manthus* at least once on every page. It could have been why I often wanted to heave the typewriter against the wall and watch its guts tinkle down among the mouse-dirt. It might have been why I typed for hours without once making sure that the back legs of the chair were not inching off the coffee table. As the weeks had passed, Rennie's notes had become more and more overscrawled, more embroidered with asterisks and elaborate instructions for reversing sentences, and each day there was a page or two less to type.

He complained easily of distractions these days, and I knew that I must not do the dishes with gusto, but furtively, placing each bowl in the rack as carefully as if it was Ming to prevent one clinking against another. I also knew I must not blow my nose inside the house, but must go outside to do it, watched in amazement by the goat. Rennie complained that the doves in the loft above him made *a terrific racket,* but there was nothing we could do about that. When Domenico shouted to the animals, or started one of his monologues in the barn, the frown on Rennie's face would deepen. He would bite his pen, and finally fling the chair back with an angry scrape that I could hear downstairs. Only when Domenico fell silent would work start again on *Malthus and the Doctrine of Necessary Catastrophe.*

I had finished typing the last page of the notes and was shuffling them together in a neat pile when I heard a rustle outside the open window in front of me and the Chinaman face of the goat blinked in. Its round eye looked at me with contempt. It stared at me and everything on the chest of drawers and then vanished from the window, but a moment later it hesitated at the front door, sniffing the air for a trap, and clopped briskly across the tiles. Ignoring me, it put its front hooves up on the coffee table and reached with whiskery lips for the roses in the jar beside the typewriter. The coarse beard wagged as it enveloped each flower in its mouth and munched before reaching for the next. It did not bother even glancing at me. It could see I was not edible. After the roses were finished it let itself back down onto the floor, where it discovered a small paper bag and was munching that, blinking, when Domenico's face appeared at the window. He exclaimed so excitely and made such histrionic gestures at the goat that a thread of spittle landed on Rennie's notes. He ran in a crouch as if under gunfire through the door towards the goat, and made a grab for the rope round the animal's neck. The goat ducked and skittered sideways, trotting round the room before leaping on to the sofa, its wicked eyes rolling at us. Domenico hissed and barked at it, finally making a lunge across the sofa and grabbing the rope with a shout.

— What's going on, what the hell's all the noise?

Rennie was still holding his pen as he stood on the stairs looking down. We all stared at each other and in the silence the goat lowered its head against the rope and let fall a few dry turds that made a light patter on the tiles. Domenico sent the goat out the door with a slap on its bony behind and scuffed the turds under the couch with the side of his boot. Then he looked up grinning.

— *Buon giorno,* he exclaimed, as if nothing had happened.

Rennie came down the last step and frowned.

— *Buon giorno,* Domenico.

Each letter was painfully distinct so that he sounded very English.

— Louise, we've got to tell him we can't have this. Domenico, *io,* er, *scrivo.*

He turned to me, making writing gestures with his pen.

— We've got to tell him.

— But darling, he was getting rid of it for us.

My words hung plaintively in the silence. When Domenico murmured *mi scusi, mi scusi,* with a placating gesture, we seemed joined, the old man and myself, against my husband. Rennie glanced from one to the other like someone cornered, then came forward. His smile was tight and there was a smear of ink on his cheek.

—Okay Domenico.

He turned to me.

—How do I say it's okay?

—*Va bene.*

—*Va bene,* Rennie repeated. How do I say thanks for getting rid of it?

I did not know either, but I was better at inventing than my husband, and made the shooing gestures Domenico had used to drive out the goat and said:

—*Grazie, grazie,* Domenico.

The inside of the old man's mouth was black and toothless when he opened it to laugh. He shuffled away with vague bowing gestures, not looking at Rennie, but grinning and bowing at me until he reached the front door. The chair that I used to prop it open caught his eye and he stopped to run a hand over the seat like a caress, and lifted it as if to judge its weight.

—*Ciao,* I called, to speed him along.

He straightened up guiltily from the chair and polished a small pane of glass between us before leaving Rennie and me alone together. Rennie flipped through the papers on the dresser.

—Sorry about that darling. I'm not cut out for that sort of thing.

He grinned and touched my hair briefly as if testing its temperature.

—You're doing a great job you know darling.

He shifted the chair closer to the centre of the coffee table.

—But watch you don't fall off this table. Has that old fruitcake made off with any more chairs lately?

As he finished speaking, Domenico's other voice rang out from the barn. The words were unclear but the tone was one of sonorous, pounding rhetoric, the kind that converts millions, and leads armies to victory in battle.

— Should we tell Hugo they're going missing? He might think we're pawning them or something.

I shook my head, but Rennie had lost interest in his question. His cheeks shook as he began to run on the spot, lifting his knees up to his chin. He ran lightly around the room, paused for an instant to give me a kiss on the cheek, and leapt up the stairs two at a time. I heard the stairway tremble under his weight and imagined a few more cracks in the risers, and the beams shifting apart another fraction of an inch. The final collapse was only a matter of time.

5

In preparation for the afternoon stroll—*mens sana, corpore sano,* Rennie often reminded me—I took the chair from against the front door and pushed it half-closed so that while we were away the goat would not come in and munch his way through *Malthus and the Doctrine of Necessary Catastrophe.* The intimidating key was still wedged in the lock from our attempts to turn it on the first day, but we had not bothered to try to get it out after we discovered that the entire lock had crumbled away, and the door yielded like an eager virgin, at a determined push.

I sat down to wait for Rennie on the bench outside, next to the sad row of dead plants in pots. In the barn, Domenico's voice was winding itself up, gathering volume in the slow acceleration towards midnight, when his voice would finally crack and fall silent. *È vero,* he was exlaiming. *È vero, è vero! Capito, sì, capito! Sì, sì, capito!* The hens in the barn clucked soothingly. When he spoke again it was in long careful phrases as if adding up all the evidence in the case for the prosecution. I watched the rooster puffing out its scrawny feathers on a wheel of the hay-wagon and gathering its breath to crow, throwing its head back so I could see the sharp bill quivering. I missed with the pebble I threw, but it hit the wagon close enough for the rooster to squawk and fluster down off the wheel and run behind the barn. That cock, arrogant on his dung-heap, was beginning to madden me with his jeering crow.

Domenico's voice was low and dramatic now, with some deadly iron-fisted threat, or the story of a mutilated corpse half-buried under the trees.

— The mice have moved that paper right away from the hole, Rennie said, appearing at the door, and I had to think what he was talking about, lost in my dream of hidden corpses.

— They must get together at night like a tug of war team.

He walked around to the side of the house, where a skeletal ground-plan of broken walls, and a crumbled pile of bricks, showed that at some time recently part of the house had gaped apart, collapsed into itself, and fallen. He climbed up on the remains of a wall and pointed.

— There's the hole. This is like a kind of staircase for them to climb up to it.

He kicked at the fallen wall, making a few more bricks collapse, and stared up at the house and the heavy grey moss hanging from the eaves.

— The whole place will go one of these days, he said, and slapped the wall as if testing it.

He jumped down, flattening blackberry fronds with his boots, brushing grit off his hands.

— Ready to go? Let's visit those two today, Hugo and what's-her-name.

Even in this warm afternoon, the wood in the valley between the two houses was as dark and clammy as a cellar. We struggled through the undergrowth, pushing against dark bushes that almost hid the path, and knocking down unravelling webs strung loosely from branch to branch. Twigs dragged at my hair, and a branch heavy with spines whipped into my chest behind Rennie. I let him thrust on ahead of me, listening to his body attacking each bush in its path like a flung-open door, and his exclamation as he slapped away some insect on his face. The square cleaver would be useful here. With that in one hand, and the heavy steel carving-knife in the other, I could make the sap run from every branch. When Rennie stopped suddenly and stood listening hard, as if to distant military music or a death-rattle in the undergrowth, the silence was full of tiny ticking sounds. There was a sly rustle on the ground that might have been nothing more than a snapped twig settling into the earth. I could hear the tightness in his voice:

—Darling, let's get a move on.

Down here in the smell of moss and the heady scent of some crushed leaf, the cuckoo's banal call was like a taunt.

On the far side of the wood, standing in the sun, we picked twigs from each other's hair and I used a leaf to remove a tiny red spider from Rennie's ear, but even when I'd patted and rubbed myself, I felt sudden pricklings on the back of my legs and neck.

—Let's go round by the road on the way back, Rennie said.

In the long field running up to the other house, he took my hand. We walked awkwardly together up through the grass, Rennie's hand dragging me forward one moment and pulling me back the next, so I found myself panting and stumbling and wanting to shake off his hand as though it was a clinging insect. I imagined Hugo and Viola standing watching our clumsy progress from behind the big windows.

—Maybe it's like the Queen, Rennie said. Flying the flag when they're at home.

Trying to feel like casual neighbours, we knocked at the back door and heard the dog bark hollowly inside the house. The desperate birds had gone, but the fishing lines were still tied to the pegs in the ground. I bent to look closer and saw a tight knot around a tiny stiff twig with

31

clenched claws. Around the pegs, the earth had been worn down into a shallow dusty dish.

Viola opened the door and stared for a moment before smiling and stepping back into the house as if to show she had nothing to hide.

— How nice, she exclaimed, and guiltily smoothed the thick dark hair across her forehead. How nice. Can I offer you a glass of wine?

As we walked into the kitchen, I could hear a steady murmur, a low drone made up of hundreds of separate sounds. It was the clocks, all of them ticking away together, each one a mass of jittering wheels beneath the bland face. Hugo joined us in the kitchen, repeating his sister's gesture of smoothing the hair across his forehead. They shared everything, it seemed, even the ritual of opening the wine: Viola wound a corkscrew into the top of a bottle and handed it to Hugo to pull out, then she held the glasses while he poured with a professional twist of the wrist. She handed me one glass, Hugo handed Rennie another, then they raised their own in a toast, smiling the half-smile they seemed to share between them.

— *Salute.*

— Cheers, Rennie replied, raising his glass. There was a pause in which he could clearly be heard swallowing.

— This is good wine, I said, feeling the need to fill the silence. Is it local?

— Yes, said Hugo, and held his glass up to the light, looking past it at me. It's from a village nearby.

— Really? Maybe you'll take us there sometime.

I saw that Rennie was also finding it necessary to make small-talk.

— I'd like to take some back with us to London.

He smiled at Hugo but it was Viola who replied.

— The best kind of *Chianti,* she said, and swirled the wine in her glass. She pointed to the emblem on the label.

—*Gallo nero,* this is what to look for. Black cockerel, black rooster.

—Black cock, said Hugo and he and his sister both took a sip of wine at the same moment as if to drown a smile. Rennie snorted and glanced at Hugo as if about to wink at him in a man-to-man way, but Hugo did not return the glance. He shifted his chair around towards me and held up the bottle.

—See?

His finger pointed at the black rooster on the label and he watched me sideways. I nodded, but he seemed to be waiting for more. Viola leaned back in her chair and stretched so hard she grew taller, then slumped down again, staring at the table with vague eyes.

—Tired? Rennie asked.

She shook her head without looking at him.

—It's this heat, he suggested.

—No, I'm not tired, she said.

She glanced at Rennie blankly, then stared across the table at Hugo, who sat twirling his glass. He was untroubled by the three of us all watching him. Viola suddenly laughed and said:

—Not tired, just fucked.

There was another kind of silence then, broken by a commotion at the door as the dog jostled in, bouncing off the door-jamb.

—Down, Iris!

At Hugo's shout, the dog squatted on the stump of its tail, shaking its head and making the chain jangle.

—Nice dog, Rennie suggested. I hoped he would not comment on the chain.

—Yes, said Hugo without interest. She's a good dog. Our mother bought her as a guard but now she has no need of her.

—Not with the Major to bark for her, Viola said, and

laughed in a shriek that she cut off with a hand over her mouth. I knew that Rennie was about to say *What Major? What mother? And why the chain?* and I knew our hosts would love the chance to make another mystery. I filled the silence with the first thought that came to me.

—I like your flags, I told Viola. They're like semaphore but I never learnt how to read it.

—Nor did we, she replied blandly. What they mean for ships is too dull for words, I suspect.

I felt as if I had flung back curtains to find a blank wall. I watched the brother and sister exchanging a look. Nothing could penetrate their secrets, unless they wanted them penetrated.

—Daniel told us to look for the flags, I said. But we got thoroughly lost anyway.

Hugo lifted the wine bottle to his lips, took a swig, and wiped his mouth on the back of his hand.

—Our father's directions were probably not very good. In some ways he's rather dumb.

Rennie laughed uncomfortably.

—Oh, I don't know . . .

I said:

—He told us to ask for Aretta, but no one knew where that was.

Hugo spluttered into his wine.

—Typical, he said, wiping his mouth. Not surprising you had trouble.

He took a long gulp of wine, leaving Viola to explain.

—Aretta is deserted, it's just ruins. No one's lived there for years.

Hugo summed it up:

—Father's just out of touch, that's all.

Rennie's voice was louder than necessary and its edge carried a small weight of annoyance as he said:

—Well, we got here, anyway.

34

Hugo and Viola leaned back in their chairs, letting his remark die in the silence. I picked up my glass to drink and had tilted it to my mouth before I realized it was empty. I could not think of any more remarks. Rennie turned to Hugo and smoothed his moustache nervously as if to try saying something more, but at that moment Viola said:

— Yes, you got here in the end. Perhaps you'd like to see the house.

She stood up and led the way out of the kitchen without waiting for an answer. Rennie followed with a backward glance at his wine — this felt like the prelude to a goodbye — and I started out of the room after them, but Hugo stopped me.

— That's boring. Let me show you my room.

His room, at the other end of the house, was large and sunny, looking over the valley towards our mouse-house. From this angle it looked like a ruin, and the collapsed bricks and tiles seemed to drag down the part still standing. I wondered how long I'd have to stand at this window staring out before I could see it all disintegrate. The mice would be buried, the knives would be covered with tons of powdery brick, and *Malthus and the Doctrine of Necessary Catastrophe* would blow about, pages freeing themselves from the rubble and fluttering into the wheat.

— This is my collection.

Hugo drew me away from the window to the dark side of the room. After the bright landscape and sky outside, the corner seemed black and I squeezed my eyes tight, seeing darkness shot with rainbows. When I opened them I saw a bench with a kind of museum exhibit of stuffed birds, all with vicious beaks and threateningly fanned wings. One bird the size of a hawk gripped a mouse in its sharp claws. Where the talons were embedded in the preserved flesh, the pale belly of the mouse was slit with a shining red gash.

—I touch them up for a more realistic look.

As my eyes adjusted, I bent closer to look at the details. A lizard hung from a heavy beak closed around it like scissors. In another sharp beak, the head and frenzied legs of a grasshopper seemed to struggle for life.

—Don't miss these.

Hugo pointed to a further bench, where snakes were coiled around dead branches. Their forked tongues seemed to flicker poisonously.

—Very lifelike.

I wondered why I was whispering.

—Not frightened, are you?

I turned to see Hugo watching my mouth.

—No, of course not.

Feeling his breath on my ear, I stared at a thick snake with a bulge the size of a fist halfway down its length.

—They swallow mice whole. They love young ones. Of course I got that effect in the mounting, but it's striking, I think.

He laughed and moved back to the window, staring out across the valley.

—From here I can keep an eye on you, Louise.

I looked over his shoulder at our house and tried to remember whether the glass in the bathroom window was frosted. I felt myself blushing as Hugo turned and watched me.

—Do you see anything interesting? I asked, to break my blushing silence.

He pursed his lips, considering.

—Oh, sometimes. Sometimes, *niente. Parli italiano?*

—Oh, *poco.*

I laughed in a way that sounded foolish to me.

—*Molto poco,* in fact.

I laughed again and wondered why I was giggling when he was not. He stared at me until I stopped, then turned away with a gesture.

— My kingdom, he said. My desk. My bed. My stamp collection.

The bed was rumpled as if from weeks of violent passion, but before I could decide whether the stamp collection was a joke, he said:

— Would you like to?

His eyes were a dark unflecked brown, so dark that the irises were invisible.

— Learn, I mean.

He waited again and blinked several times while I licked my lips and wondered.

— Italian, of course.

With a sudden theatrical swoop he took my hand and went down on one knee, declaiming in Italian. I wondered whether this had all been planned in advance, and stared at the place like a navel on the crown of his head, from which all the hair grew. I could imagine it very easily, passion in the secret hot centre of a wheat field. When he stood up and dropped my hand it was as indifferently as if he'd been tying his shoelace.

— Great language, he said.

He turned to the window and stared across the valley towards the other house. I thought he was shading his eyes from the glare but when I moved closer beside him I saw that he had made circles of his fingers and was looking through them like binoculars. I wondered again about that glass.

— *Allora*. The others will be thinking we've eloped.

He turned away from the window and led the way back to the kitchen. There was still no sign of Viola or Rennie, and I found myself glancing up at the ceiling, waiting to hear a shoe fall to the floor above. Hugo took a long drink

of wine from the bottle and wiped carelessly at the drops
that spilled down his shirt.

— I want to show you something, Louise.

Again I thought of secret passion and glanced guiltily
towards the door. Hugo caught my glance and said flatly:

— It's in here.

He opened the freezing compartment of the refrigerator
and took out a small brown-paper package.

— See if you can guess, Louise, what this is.

I felt that something serious was involved in guessing
right, and I was determined to pass the test. Hugo seemed
someone it would be hard to surprise, and I was determined, after all that blushing and giggling and being
foolish, to surprise him. I took the frozen bundle, which
had no particular shape beyond being thicker in the
middle than at the ends. I held it to my ear and shook
it, smiling at Hugo, but he would not play my game, only
his own. The bundle did not rattle and he did not smile
back.

— All this wrapping, I said and pouted. It's not fair.

He shrugged.

— You know all you need to guess.

I was suddenly sick of all the obscurities in this house,
and started to rip the paper away from the bundle, but
Hugo grabbed it from me. When Viola and Rennie came
in, I could not have said whether Hugo and I had been
staring at each other with the bundle between us for a
second or an hour. Viola looked at the bundle, at me,
then at her brother. With some significant kind of smile,
she said sweetly:

— Showing our secrets, are you?

Rennie crossed the room and watched as Hugo
unwrapped the bundle quickly and showed its contents
to him like an Egyptian with dirty postcards under his
coat. I was so obviously excluded that I turned away and
caught a wink between Viola and Hugo.

38

— You must come and see us again, Viola said quickly as if to smother the wink. Look for the flags, when there are several up it means a good mood.

Hugo let out a whooping laugh. I saw Rennie laugh too, glancing from Hugo to Viola, and I wanted to shout, can't you see we're not supposed to understand? Don't you see this is a nasty private game?

As I walked down the driveway with Rennie, I felt that the brother and sister were watching our backs. I glanced back once, and Hugo took his hand from around his sister's waist and waved hugely, mockingly, like a fond uncle. Until we turned through the gate into the road, I continued to feel them staring at our backs, and imagined the whispered remarks they would be exchanging until we were out of hearing, and the screams of hilarity at our expense later that would make Iris bark madly.

We walked back along the road, watching the sun expand milkily as it slid down towards the hills behind the house.

— Those two are pretty weird, Rennie said loudly into the evening. Daniel's such a good fellow, odd his children turned out like that.

I said nothing, but walked backwards for a few steps, looking at the two small flags fluttering above the trees. Rennie became more insistent.

— Don't you think?

I glanced at his heavy face, its every pore exposed in the last rays of sun.

— Yes.

I thought of those two, companionable now over the wine in the kitchen, sharing their jokes.

— What was in the package?

Rennie kicked a stone along in front of him.

— Bit peculiar, some kind of bird. Frozen, you know, with the feathers and everything.

I concentrated on keeping out of step with him, walking in the other rut of the road.

—Can't imagine why he thought I'd want to see it.

I stopped and let him draw ahead, watching his broad back move steadily, obliviously, up the road. I wondered how long it would take, if I turned and walked back down the road, for him to be aware that I was no longer beside him. What would I say, exactly, when Viola opened the door with a glass of wine in her hand, staring in polite dismay?

—Listen, Rennie said. What happened . . .

He turned and stared at his shoes, waiting for me to catch up.

—What were you doing with Hugo all that time? That nutty sister was up to something, too.

I still said nothing.

—Lou, what the hell's the matter?

He stood in the road with his hands in his pockets and his face thrust towards me, angry and alarmed in the direct light.

—He showed me his display.

Rennie's face flushed, or perhaps it was the red glow of the sun.

—His what?

—Stuffed birds and things. Like a museum.

I thought of the overgrown navel on Hugo's head and his stern face as he stared through the imaginary binoculars. Rennie and I walked in silence. I glanced around at the trees and heard invisible birds tweeting and screeching in them. I was dizzy, feeling how easily this landscape could stagger crookedly into the sky, reel in on itself, freeze and sliver apart in long shards. We continued to plod in silence and although I kept pace beside Rennie, I imagined the sudden spurt of dust and the feeling of the breeze on my face if I tucked my elbows in to my sides and sprinted away, leaving him behind.

On the last stretch of road, where it followed the spine of the ridge, the darkening air suddenly filled with darting shapes around our heads. I watched as one of the tiny birds streaked across in front of me and stopped dead in the air, suspended for an instant in which I could see the long flukes of a swallow's tail, before it took off again, drawing another straight line in the sky. The birds were coming at us from all directions, blurred with speed, hissing like whips around our faces.

—What is this? Rennie said in confusion, standing with a halo of midges around his head.

I watched as three blurs converged on him, watched him duck and cringe as if he thought they were knives flying through the air. I knew the birds were not attacking us, but I could guess, too, that in the dusk an eyeball might seem as juicy a morsel as a midge. Rennie was crouching with his hands up protecting his face. He would stagger backwards, screaming, his hands over the blood pouring down his cheek, and stand waiting for me to run over and help him to the house, with my arm around his shoulders and soothing words in his ear.

—Cover your eyes, darling, he said in a high voice, and began to trot up the road out of the mist of midges, waving me on with one hand and shielding his face with the other. His fear made me fearless, and I let him disappear around the corner of the barn, following slowly, shuffling my sandals through the drifts of dust on the side of the road, delaying the return. The sun had set now behind the hills and the sky was full of long shreds of cloud all drawn like hairs down a plughole towards the glow on the horizon left by the sun.

As I passed Domenico's barn, I wondered if he had been shouting as Rennie and I came up the road, and whether he was watching, waiting for us to go into the house before starting again. The barn seemed too silent, the split and peeling shutters sealed too tightly on the window. In there, Domenico's eyes would be accustomed to the dark, and anyone walking across the yard would be exposed in every detail to him as he peered through the chinks, breathing quietly, watching. I glanced at the shutters and had to look away in case I might be staring straight into his unblinking eyes. I scuffed a clump of straw along in front of me, making a noise in case he was sniggering at me as I passed. I could imagine his face distorted in the gloom and the whispered Italian obscenities as he watched me walk in front of him. I winced as a hen darted out in front of me and ran frantically ahead, flapping its wings against its sides as if I was coming after it with a knife.

The house was very dark as I approached the front door, propped open again by Rennie, and I stood feeling the current of cool air from inside. In the loft the doves were murmuring soothingly to each other. I could see a glimmering white shape in the opening above me, and imagined the smelly warmth up there, and the odd white feather dislodged from the armpit of a wing and floating down. It was calming, standing there listening to that happy family, and I wondered how I would ever make myself go back into the dark house.

6

Inside the house everything was rushing and humming with a flow of water. Upstairs I knew Rennie was in the shower, soaping himself over and over, standing with the hair streaming down his forehead, lathering between his legs with a look of satisfaction. I had watched him alone with his own body, and knew how happy it made him look. I was prickling and itching all over and as soon as the water stopped flowing I went up to the steamy bathroom. Rennie did not look at me as I came in and took my clothes off, but continued his methodical drying of each toe with his foot towel as if he was still alone in the room.

— I'm itching all over, I said loudly, so he could not pretend not to hear me, and stepped into the shower-stall. He said nothing and I said:

— As if I've been rolling in hay.

— What? Rennie said irritably. I can't hear you.

— Rolling in hay, I repeated.

— Spoiling the day? What do you mean?

He thrust open the shower-curtain and I wanted to cover my nakedness, perhaps because it was invisible to him.

— Nothing, darling, I said.

He looked at me expressionlessly, then turned to show me his shoulderblade.

— Do I have a bite or something here?

The flesh of his back was soft and steamy and I thought how the skin could be pulled off smoothly along that

43

translucent membrane between skin and flesh, leaving the bunched muscles exposed like an anatomist's model.

— Nothing.

He moved away to the mirror and I closed the curtain again. His crinkly hairs were stuck to the soap and I held it under the water, rubbing at it until all the hairs had washed away. I did not want my husband's hairs on my body. I listened to the silence beyond the curtain, which seemed to be more than just silence, but was loud with reproach or annoyance. Hearing him rustle and sigh and the snap of elastic against flesh, I parted the shower-curtain and looked out. The big window in front of which Rennie was bending was made of clear glass. Like this, at night, with darkness all around, from outside the room would appear lit like a stage, and Rennie the main actor for any audience that might be out there.

I pulled the curtain closed, feeling the hot water gush over my shoulders, and closed my eyes, thinking about hot wheat fields and the way hair grew from the crown of a head. The temperature of the water was the same as inside myself, so that my fingers slid in and out and there was pleasure in not knowing where I began and ended. I was smiling under the water, leaning backwards against the wall and losing myself in pleasure, when my thumb felt something hard in my pubic hair. Suddenly I was drowning in all this hot water, rushing over my mouth and nose and blinding me with my own hair. The lump, like a scab, could not be pulled or scraped off with a fingernail and in panic I bent forward and tried to put my head between my legs to look at whatever it was. Water poured over the back of my head and up my nose, and my hair streamed forward and hid everything.

Rennie was gone from the bathroom when I stepped out and squatted on the floor, still dripping, and held the hand mirror between my legs. The mirror kept steaming

44

up and drops of water landed on it, but each time I wiped it clear for a moment I saw something small and black and possibly moving, something that felt alive, definitely alive but embedded in my skin, something firmly attached but not a part of me.

Naked, I ran into the embryo room next door where Rennie was sitting at the desk pushing back his cuticles. He glanced around and his eyes flickered over my body.

— Rennie, there's something stuck to me. I can't see.

— Something what?

Rennie frowned at me as if listening to a stammerer.

— It's here.

I put one leg up on a chair and felt the spot with my finger.

— Look.

He peered cautiously between my legs.

— No, here.

I pointed to the right spot and he bared his teeth with surprise and disgust.

— It's a tick.

He looked at me in horror. He was quite pale.

— It's gone a long way in. I'll have to dig it out.

He did not look at me again or touch me before he went into the bathroom and returned with tweezers and alcohol.

— Better lie down.

He spread a towel on one of the beds. As he worked in my skin, his lips were drawn back in revulsion at what he was doing. The alcohol stung and I felt the sharp ends of the tweezers gouging my flesh, but I stared at the ceiling and forced myself to be calm. Rennie was silent as he worked but finally he straightened up and said:

— Think I got it all. It's bleeding a bit but I think I got it all out.

After a quick glance at my face he took the equipment

back to the bathroom. I shuddered and felt gooseflesh rise all over my body. When Rennie came back I was running my fingers through my hair to feel every inch of scalp.

— I can't see my back, would you check?

He watched as I ran a finger down the cleft of my buttocks. His laugh was as brash as a trumpet fanfare when he said:

— Think you might have a whole family of them?

His voice was so loud and insistent that I wanted to cover my ears against it. I had a headache now, and wondered whether it was from the tension of the last half-hour, or whether the tick was already poisoning my system.

In the bedroom I dressed slowly, hearing Rennie sneeze three times from his desk but deciding not to say *Bless you darling* and hear him reply, *Thank you darling*. I made no noise going downstairs and wondered how long it would take him to realize I was no longer in the house.

Yellow light could be seen now between the chinks of Domenico's shutters, and a strip of ground outside the door was lit up. I moved over towards the shutters and heard rustlings from the room inside, and an occasional grunt. Both the barn and the house were very black against the still-pale sky and I stood for a long time watching the air darken and the silhouettes of the buildings dissolve. At such a time of the day, when objects could melt, I felt serene, and could imagine anything might be possible.

Domenico's voice suddenly rang out: *Non è possibile! Non è possibile!* I had never heard him from such close range, and strained to interpret the noises I could hear beneath the words. I held my breath and felt congested from the thought of his discovering me, but I took a few steps closer to the window. To be able to look through the crack that ran across the shutter, I would have to climb on something. There was sudden complete silence from inside, and I hardly breathed, waiting. When the silence was broken again with clattering and scraping noises, Domenico shouted so angrily that I was sure I'd been spotted. *Apri! Apri la bocca!* I was afraid this was abuse, aimed at the eavesdropping foreigner, but his shouting dwindled to a hoarse whisper: *Ecco, ecco, ecco,* and I took courage again. I picked up a fruit box by the wall and crept to the window with it, moving only when he spoke and freezing in mid-movement when he was silent. I waited for more shouts: *Aspetta! Aspetta!* before stepping onto the box, and as I did so I felt a deep dragging spasm in my belly. Standing on the box in another silence, I waited impatiently for more shouting, then pulled my skirt up and thrust a hand inside my underpants. Domenico fell silent again and I stood bent over the box, with two fingers as far up inside myself as they could go. When he started again: *Basta, basta cosi, basta!* he sounded at his last gasp. I withdrew my fingers and inspected them in the light from the crack in the shutter. Along one fingernail and as far down as the first joint there was a dark smear. Letting my skirt drop back into place I stared up into the sky and released the sigh that had been building up inside me for an eternity.

Finiscila! Finiscila! Being careful not to let the box creak under my weight, I leaned forward until I could see into the yellow-lit stone room. At first I saw only chairs, at least a dozen of them, lined up and facing the window. I recognized three that had disappeared from the house. For a moment, seeing the chairs all facing me, I thought I was somehow on a stage, and pulled back in fright before I peered again, even more carefully this time. With the limited field of view I had, I could not see Domenico and thought for a moment he had crept out of the barn and was behind me, watching silently as I crouched and peered. But the dark yard was empty when I turned to look, and when I heard him muttering inside the room I squinted sideways through the crack, guided by the sound of his voice. By flattening my face against the peeling paint and closing one eye, I could just make out a pair of boots at the end of stretched-out legs and realized that Domenico was sitting on the floor with his back to the wall I was leaning against.

I continued to watch, and saw what was causing the clattering and scraping when I saw the goat's hindquarters back slowly into my line of sight, the legs scrabbling as if the animal was pulling against a rope. *Basta, basta, basta.* Domenico's voice was a tired mumble. The goat stayed still, the boots did not move, and I was losing interest and was about to get down from the box when a hen strayed into the room and pecked myopically at a trail of straw under the chairs. Domenico leapt into full view, kicking at the flustered hen until it found the doorway again and disappeared into the dark barn beyond. I only just had time to jump down from the box and move it away from the window before Domenico came outside, followed by the goat. I hoped I looked as if I had just emerged from the house for an evening stroll.

—*Buona sera,* Domenico.

He came towards me, grinning toothlessly, and said a few quick sentences with many gestures.

—Um . . . *prego?*

He spoke again, and this time I caught two names.

—Hugo? Viola?

Domenico came closer so that the light from the cracked shutter lit him up like a saint, grinning and winking as he spoke again. I shrugged and smiled in response, not caring much, light-headed with the knowledge of my freedom. Impatient now, Domenico gestured hugely and mouthed at me, pointing across the valley to the lights of the other house.

—Hugo. Viola.

I nodded. He repeated his long sentence, but it still meant nothing to me. His mouth let out a cackle without changing shape and I caught a whiff of something rank and animal. He held up his hands and watched me closely as he made a circle with the thumb and forefinger of his left hand, and pushed the forefinger of his right hand in and out of this circle, watching me understand.

—*Capisce?* Hugo. Viola.

He winked at me and laughed raspily. I laughed too and felt a warm spurt between my legs. Domenico watched me through his cackling as if he knew, nodding and winking at me as I stood laughing in the dusk, dizzy with possibility.

7

Upstairs, Rennie was still at his desk in the embryo room. He did not hear me as I climbed up onto the double bed and lay staring at the ceiling beams, a hand on my belly. I heard him tear up a sheet of paper and clear his throat, then turned over on my side, feeling the warm ooze between my legs, and pulled a pillow over my head. There were decisions to be made, now that I was restored to myself, decisions about greed and vanity, and the shapes a life might take when restored to choice, but I did not want to make any of them just yet.

I had been dreaming comfortably of a big green parrot pecking at an ornate table when Rennie shook me awake. Seeing his pale shocked face I sat up quickly.

— What is it?

Rennie got up on the bed and tucked his feet under the pillow.

— There's a snake, he whispered hoarsely. In the room, I saw its tail go under the bed. You know, where the mice . . .

The words came woodenly through his stiff lips and I saw from a great unconcerned distance that his eyes were blank with fear.

— It's been there all the time, he whispered. All the time. I've been sitting there and it's been right there. All the time.

I stared at him, watching his fear, which made me calm. When I slid down from the bed and felt another spasm in my belly, I knew I could take charge of any amount of life.

—Put your shoes on, I said. And pull your socks over the cuffs of your pants.

I shook the galoshes in the wardrobe and pulled them on while he dragged his socks up. I ran downstairs and returned to the bedroom with two brooms. Rennie was still sitting in the middle of the bed, pale and staring.

—That hole, I said, my mind throwing up pictures as clear as snapshots. The one we thought was a mouse hole. Must be the snake's. We can scare him out through it and then block it properly.

My words seemed to ring through the room and buffet Rennie as he stood swaying and staring at me with his mouth ajar. When Domenico suddenly shouted from the barn his voice seemed to echo my own.

I led the way into the embryo room, half hoping to see the snake slip out from under the bed and spend its venom striking at the rubber of my boots. Rennie took up position on the other side of the room, as far from the bed as possible. I did not tell him he was in front of the hole in the wall. I bent to look under the bed and waited till my eyes had adjusted to the darkness under there, imagining the quick black streak across the floor, the sudden high scream from Rennie, myself rolling back the sock and seeing the two small holes in his ankle. The dark blot I could see now must be the snake.

—Careful Louise. Careful.

I glanced at Rennie and saw him grip the broom tighter, holding it out in front of him as if to impale an attacker. His face was waxy and seemed to have shrunk. Would the long knife be the best to lance the two poisoned holes, its own weight as it fell across the flesh helping any last-minute faintness of heart I might suffer? Or perhaps the slim bendy one, the sharpest of all, for two quick slashes? Or perhaps the bite of the serrated one? The tiny teeth would cut through his flesh like a chainsaw through sappy wood.

— I'm going to poke it, I said. It might go for the hole.

As I jabbed the broom handle towards the dark shadow I saw out of the corner of my eye that Rennie had realized the danger of his position. He stepped quickly sideways and looked for something to climb on. I would have to hold the ankle in my lap so he could not see what I was doing, and keep the knives hidden from him. After the quick cuts the wounds would not bleed for a moment and I would see grey beads of cartilage before blood would begin to flow everywhere. Just before he climbed on the chair I poked hard at the dark shape under the bed. I jumped back and heard him gasp. The dark shape did not move, there was no dark streak towards the hole. Watching it this time, I jabbed again, jabbed and poked and pulled until the dirty blue shirt was lying at my feet.

— Oh my god, said Rennie. It could be anywhere.

Still standing on the chair, he lifted the broomstick off the floor as if the snake might suddenly dart out from somewhere and shinny up it. My feet were hot and sweaty in the galoshes and I felt the blood sticky between my legs.

— It's probably already gone.

I went around the room carefully poking the broom under the other bed, separating the newspapers shuffled together in the corner, finally shaking both mattresses so hard that the family under the plastic milled frantically and the embryos writhed over each other.

— It's okay, I said. Gone for sure.

I took the brick Rennie used to keep the door open and put it against the hole.

— Locked out.

Rennie stepped down from the chair and tapped the broom handle against the floor.

— Or locked in.

He bit his lips and we stood watching each other, hearing the secretive scratching of the mice in the mattress.

Domenico's voice carried clearly in through the window. The crowd was on its feet, waving banners, throwing caps in the air, and above it the voice gathered into a sonorous climax before it was drowned in wave after wave of cheers.

8

I had met Daniel once in London, after Rennie had triumphantly delivered the Malthus Memorial Lecture. I had sat at the other end of a long table at dinner later, watching him lean towards Rennie, clinking his glass and patting his back and shoulders. *Fine job, my dear boy,* I had heard him exclaim, and I had watched him pat and pat my husband as if he could not make himself stop.

In the living room of the house his children lived in, with a view across the valley to our mouse-house, I wondered just who Daniel was. He had arrived from London only hours before, but already looked as if he had never set foot outside his Italian estate. I wondered whether he had always been as neat as a clockwork cat, or whether marriage to the elegant *signora* had done it. Her portrait, full of the glitter of diamonds, dominated the room, but Daniel never looked at it. It was possible that he had grown up familiar with the bread-and-dripping of a meagre childhood, stepping over vomit in East End gutters on Saturday nights. His coin-smooth face, polished rather than flawed by the passage of his fifty years, could be the response to a fat mother who'd shouted so hard when she was angry that the metal curlers on her head shook like the castanets of a Salvation Army tambourine.

— Well. Well. Well.

He thrust his hands deep into the pockets of his jacket and rocked back on his heels, staring at me as if inspecting my neck for a bath-ring.

—It's very kind . . . I began automatically. I expected
him to interrupt my thanks with a wave of the hand, but
he stood smiling tidily until I'd found my way to the end
of my little speech. Nodding in approval, he turned to
Rennie.

—My dear boy, I insist that you admire the miracles
Hugo and Viola have performed in the garden.

With a hand on Rennie's arm, he led him to the huge
window that filled one wall and overlooked the valley of
the cuckoos. I stood beside them while Daniel pointed
out the orderly details of cherry tree, grapevine, and
clipped shrub. When the dusk deepened he touched a
switch and the view of the garden was replaced like a slide
in a lecture by a black square in which the three of us
stared at each other's reflections. I could imagine neat
lettering underneath: *Variations of Physical Structure in
Homo Sapiens.* When I met Daniel's eyes in the reflection,
he turned away.

—Why are we all dying of thirst? he asked peevishly,
and vanished into the next room.

—Great place, isn't it, Rennie said, the words muffled
as he bent towards his reflection to finger a flaw beside
his mouth. He's a fascinating man, too.

He tugged at his tweed until the reflection met with his
approval and caught my eye as he brushed off his
shoulders.

—He's been a good friend to me over the years. And
he likes you, you know.

Daniel returned with tiny glasses of a liquid the colour
of urine. For a moment we all held our glasses and bowed
our heads like communicants.

—To old friends, Daniel toasted, and drained his glass.
Oh, and new ones too, of course, he added quickly, and
nodded to me.

Rennie took a sip and made a surprised noise.

— Thought it was sherry.

Daniel refilled the glasses all round and explained that it was holy wine, the *vinsanto* the Pope drank. He overfilled Rennie's glass, and bent down to take a few sips from it before handing it to him.

— They grow it nearby.

He touched Rennie's glass with his own again and said:

— What a good idea it was to come. Such a lot to see. And it's been a year since I saw the children.

Hugo and Viola had disappeared tonight without explanation, and I had noticed that the flagpole was bare. Daniel turned to me with an exaggerated effort to include me in the conversation that made me want to tiptoe out of the room.

— Since you're an artist, Louise, we'll have to make a trip to see some famous frescoes. It's a pleasant little trip and we can stay overnight in the monastery.

The night of the lecture in London, when Daniel had shakcn my hand and told me how pleased he was to meet me, he had asked:

— And what keeps you out of mischief, Louise?

Before I'd had time to answer, Rennie had said:

— Louise is at the Slade.

Now I sipped too often from my tiny glass as Daniel murmured across the room in a voice not quite loud enough to hear, and I did not like to ask *Pardon? Pardon?* too many times, so Daniel could have been murmuring about the clay they used in Tuscan plaster and its effect on frescoes, or about the previous owner of this house. He seemed to be saying that he'd been arrested for molesting his own daughter.

Rennie took advantage of his old friendship to ignore all this, and strolled around the room examining the spiders in blocks of perspex, and the Venus fly-trap in whose lips someone had just placed a dead bug. When

Daniel had tired of his whispering game he called across to Rennie:

— Reynold, you remember Spry, the one with the somewhat hairy back? I heard he was killed crossing the street.

He guffawed.

— He was a bit on the slow side, in spite of his name.

Rennie laughed, but looked down at his feet as if ashamed.

— And your beautiful mother, how is she? Daniel went on.

— She thinks the nurses are trying to make off with her jewellery. You know, those pearls.

This time Rennie could laugh with pleasure. It had been my strong impression, gained over one slow evening with her, that her pearls and her son were all that had ever mattered to Mrs Dufrey. I had admired the collection of pearls of all shapes, sizes, and colours — *Just a little hobby,* Mrs Dufrey had said rather grandly — and had done my best to remain responsive throughout the photograph album. I had prepared a solemn look when the page opened to reveal Rennie's long-dead father, but Mrs Dufrey — she had not suggested that I call her anything but Mrs Dufrey — had flipped on impatiently. She had smoothed with her finger those photographs in which a young and elegant Margaret Dufrey had looked on, smiling, as the young boy with the large head, in the Eton jacket with the corner of white handkerchief poking out of the pocket, had recited with appropriate gestures at Prize Days, danced for aunts and uncles, and dined elaborately with his *Maman.* The photograph of them lunching together showed Mrs Dufrey's long pearl earrings resting on her son's hair as they nestled up to each other for the man behind the camera. *Luncheon at Adolpho's, June 1952,* Mrs Dufrey's immaculate copperplate stated underneath. Her fountain pen — she could not bear to use anything but her gold-nibbed fountain pen — had been freshly filled and the letters stood out dark and thick on the rough paper.

Daniel turned to me, staring at me challengingly as he said:

—She's one of the most wonderful women I know.

I nodded several times, remembering the way Mrs Dufrey's plucked eyebrows had risen at each remark I had made, and how she had watched closely as I had picked up my knife and fork at dinner. Daniel became even more categorical.

—She's just magnificent.

I coughed and searched for my handkerchief until Daniel stopped staring at me and led the way downstairs.

In the dining room, where the whisper of the twenty-four clocks could be heard through the archway that led to the kitchen, I watched Daniel lay food and plates on the table. I saw that I would be clearly visible under the glass-topped table and would not be able to claw off my shoes with my toes, clench my fists in my lap, or scrawl obscenities on my knee. When he placed a huge pottery dish on the glass I made a mental note to refuse salad. The bowl could slip out of my hands and smash the table to glittering shards around our feet.

—Now, Daniel cried. The *pièce de résistance!*

He drew Rennie through the archway into the kitchen, where an olive-green lobster was sidling over wet sacking in the sink. The long feelers rotated through space and the claws opened and closed slowly on nothing. It seemed to know it was about to die.

—Watch now.

Daniel pulled me closer so I could feel the steam from the pot of water boiling on the stove.

—Watch this.

As Daniel pulled a padded mitten over one hand, the lobster began crawling slowly backwards. The feelers swivelled faster and the tail curled over its back as if in this moment of extremity the lobster was doing its best to become a scorpion. Daniel's hand snapped it up and dropped it into the boiling water in one quick movement. I winced back from the little splash, but I felt his hand on the back of my neck forcing me to look down into the pot. His grip was surprisingly strong.

—Look.

The lobster sank quickly through the water, its legs flailing slowly. It settled on the bottom and there was a scream like a wet finger drawn across glass. The lobster rose high on its legs and scuttled to the side of the pot, where it tapped urgently on the metal with its front claws. It turned clumsily and scrabbled across to the other side, moving now in feeble spastic jerks, the shriek still floating up in the steam. It seemed to take hours to die. When its legs had finally slipped and scraped weakly over the metal for the last time and the shell had turned bright red, Daniel released my neck and I felt the air cool the steam that had condensed on my face. With a hand over my mouth, I walked stiffly past Rennie, found a bathroom, and locked myself in.

At the table I allowed Daniel to heap my plate with salad but could not look at the split and steaming lobster. Daniel chuckled and gave me cheese. I kept my knees carefully together and my hands above the table as I sat toying with lettuce leaves and Rennie brought Daniel up to date while glass after glass of wine was poured.

—Malthus is a tremendously fascinating character and they've given me a fair advance. It should do pretty well they think.

Daniel drew out a long fibre of meat from a claw.

—First-rate, my dear boy. I'll soon be calling you Doctor Dufrey.

Rennie cracked a leg with a sharp noise and laughed.

—I'll get it finished this summer, but I won't demand my title until next year.

Daniel rolled up a lettuce leaf like a sock and popped it into his mouth.

—And Louise, what is keeping you out of mischief?

Rennie answered quickly as he had once before:

—Louise has been at the Slade.

—Oh!

Daniel still seemed unaware that this was a conversation having its second run, and his eyebrows arched. As if to reward me for surprising him, he offered me the olives. When I refused he sucked hard on a leg with a whistling sound and spoke through shreds of meat.

—The Slade, eh. Great men have passed through the portals there. And great boys have become great men at the Slade.

He turned to me and toasted me before tipping his head back and gulping his wine.

—May you be worthy, Louise, of those after whom you follow.

I started to explain that I had not been at the Slade as either a student or teacher of art, but Rennie interrupted to say what a *first-rate amanuensis* I was, so that for the second time I was unable to make it clear that I had only been at the Slade as a typist in the back room, where art was just a heady smell of turps.

I sat watching my knees through the table while Daniel and Rennie discussed all that had befallen Spry, Ellis, Mantova, and the rest from the old days.

—All the ones who were any good moved on to greater things. Others, such as poor Spry, never learned.

Daniel nodded at me as if poor Spry was a close friend he expected me to defend.

—Spry was somewhat slow, in spite of his name.

The second time around the joke was even less funny. I stared above Rennie's nodding head at a painting of a dead rabbit hanging by its feet from a hook.

— But my dear boy, the pleasure's all mine!

Daniel reached across the table to pat Rennie's arm.

— I'm honoured to feel that anything of mine could be useful to you in finishing the book.

Rennie ripped a piece of bread and chewed modestly.

— The other house is painfully rustic, but probably a first-class place to write. I'll come over tomorrow and see how you're managing.

He turned to me and spoke with his eyes on the scraps on my plate as if about to reach over and snatch the lettuce stem.

— And Louise, I'm sure you'll find no end of charming Italian subjects to paint. Or perhaps you use crayons?

The cuff of Rennie's jacket caught the edge of his plate and it dropped on to the table with a clatter.

— Sorry. How long are you here for, exactly?

— Oh, a month or four. My dear Reynold, are you anxious to see me go, when I've only just arrived?

We all laughed at this good joke and I wondered how much longer we would have to sit over the corpse of our tortured lobster. I wondered if I had spoken my thoughts aloud when Daniel got up and began to usher us to the door. At the front door he embraced Rennie at length.

— Dear boy, wonderful to see you again.

— Tremendous, Rennie murmured over Daniel's shoulder and winked at me.

Daniel released him with a final pat on the back and turned to me almost in time to see me wink back at Rennie.

— Delighted to meet you again, Louise.

I felt his fingertips pressing painfully into my side as he stood between his guests with an arm around each of

61

our waists. He stared out the door at the night as if trying to decide whether to thrust us apart or bang our heads together, and when he pushed us towards the door it was if to remove a temptation.

— Since you won't spend the night, off with you!

I felt him watching us as we crunched down the driveway. I imagined that from his point of view the couple walking on opposite sides of the gravel with their heads bowed might have been watching for buried explosives. At the bend in the driveway, I turned to wave goodnight but at that moment Daniel stepped inside and closed the door with a bang that set a bird screeching in a tree.

9

Since I had closed the door quietly on it, the heap of dead-white bird-droppings in the upstairs room seemed to have grown, and when he visited us, Daniel scuffed at it with his sandal. He leaned out of the blank hole of the window like someone being sick over the rail of a boat, then dusted his hands together and looked up at the rotten beams of the ceiling. He glanced at me accusingly, but said nothing until he had drawn me out of the room and closed the door quietly behind us.

— I had no idea. This is horribly dangerous.

Last night over dinner, Daniel could have been mistaken for an Italian, with his fine suits and the kid shoes from *a little man in Fiesole,* but here in the mouse-house he wore his shirt sleeves rolled up to the elbows like an English yeoman, and in spite of the considerable heat he did not appear to sweat.

— It could have been a tragedy.

He continued to stare at me in the dim hallway, where dust-motes hung in a beam of thick yellow sunlight. I found that if I stared long enough at the sunlight, Daniel's face was invisible when I looked at it again.

— You'll have to join us in the other house.

I tried to point out how strong the bricks of the walls still were, and suggested the house was safe from collapse as long as it was full of the mice. Daniel smiled at my ingenuity, but shook his head and talked about his *responsibilities*. When he suggested the move, Rennie seemed prepared to pack up instantly. No one mentioned the snake.

63

Hidden in powdery golden dust, Hugo bounced across the field on his tractor with the hay-wagon in tow. The wagon skittered crookedly across the yard and when it stopped, the big squashy tyres melted between the cobblestones. As we loaded our possessions, Rennie and I found that one of us had to stand on guard and prod the goat away with a stick, otherwise its whiskery black lips would nibble at the food, the shoes, even the books. Domenico stood in the strip of shade beside the barn, hands in pockets, winking at me every time he caught my eye, and I wondered whether his conversations would blossom now that he had the place to himself again. Perhaps he would fall silent altogether. When Daniel spoke sternly to him, Domenico straightened against the wall and took his hands out of his pockets. He even went so far as to lift my galoshes into the wagon, but his face was swallowed in the wink he gave me as soon as Daniel turned away.

When Rennie and I arrived from the mouse-house, dusty from our trip across the fields, Hugo and Viola politely repeated, rather too often, how pleased they were at the arrangement and how it really did not disturb them in the least. I found it difficult to meet their eyes and wondered how they would manage now their house had been so thoroughly invaded. It was possible, of course, that they had always been outdoor lovers. They did not have much to say to Daniel, but always ushered him first through doorways, and insisted that he have the first taste of the wine or the last sausage.

The first night, Rennie and I found it hard to fall sleep in the unfamiliar bed, and at dawn we were jerked out of sleep by a booming Italian voice. I leapt out of bed, wrapping the sheet around myself and preparing to *assume the position* against the wall, or be kidnapped or shot. Rennie blinked and said over and over again: *What is it, what is it,* and combed his hair back with his fingers as if to see better. The voice brayed on until I realized there was no raid, no fire, no revolution, but a speaker on the wall sending out deafening radio. I straightened up slowly from the wall and worked out that it was some kind of cheery breakfast show. Just as I realized this, the radio was switched off and I lay shivering next to Rennie until it was time to go down to breakfast, wishing for the mouse-house and its rotten beams.

At breakfast no one mentioned the radio until finally I admitted, when pressed—*you look tired, Louise, did you sleep badly?*—that I had not slept well. Hugo was full of effusive apologies then across the imported marmalade, and explained that he had turned on his radio and forgotten that the connected speaker in his father's room was switched on. It seemed a good joke. Everyone laughed, and Viola poured more coffee all round as if in celebration. I was sick of everyone laughing at things that were not funny, hated this house and our hosts, and wished I could roar out a yodel of rage and up-end the table. I could imagine the way the white cups would shatter and tinkle on the tiled floor as everyone goggled at me.

Hugo did not resemble his father at all, and neither did Viola. I assumed they must take after their mother, who was never mentioned in Daniel's presence. Hugo laughed loudly at all his father's jokes, and sometimes laughed when there did not seem to have been a joke at all. Viola was never seen in down-at-heel slippers or an egg-spotted dressing-gown, but was always in a state of full dress. None of her smiles seemed to be directed towards anyone in particular and her cooking was secretive. She prepared all the meals alone, refusing my help.

—Won't be for long, Rennie reassured me. Malthus will be done soon.

In fact, work on the book was progressing slowly, and I had plenty of time on my hands in the long afternoons. I would watch Rennie do his exercises before and after his run, wondering if the thick veins that wound like jungle vines up his arms would ever burst, and sometimes I would do a few toe-touches with him. Daniel usually joined us too. He had a series of small jokes about how muscular Rennie's bulky thighs were in their running shorts, and how the reddish hair was worn off at the knees and calves.

— Have you been shaving them, dear boy?

He also joked about his own thin body and dark-haired sinewy legs when he appeared in brand-new running shorts one day. It became part of the ritual of the day for Rennie and Daniel to run together in the mornings, and puff back in time for breakfast.

In the afternoons the house became very quiet. Rennie sat in state at the glass dining table, staring into space over his notes, and the other members of the household vanished like steam, reconstituting themselves later when the sun was huge and red and the first of many drinks were poured.

In those long afternoons, when I had typed the little there was to type, I wandered around the house and garden. Sometimes I came across Hugo in my wanderings. I would find him whistling scratchily through his teeth, working at some small piece of carpentry, or clipping Iris's toenails while her eyes rolled back into her head. Once he pointed to a small squat figure he had just carved. When I picked it up to look more closely, the top shot up in my hand and a chunky polished penis struck out at me. Hugo laughed his private laugh and I wondered again about what Domenico had seemed to tell me. There were times when I was sure Domenico's message had been only an invention of my own mind.

After dinner, Hugo often suggested I take a walk with him to hear a certain nightingale. I was conscious that everyone was watching me until I shook my head no. On the nights when he stayed at the table after dinner, he spoke to me at length about the fine points of bird-mounting, and the various ways to avoid mildew in stuffed animals, while I leaned away from him trying in vain to hear what Daniel was saying to Rennie. Viola always left the table as soon as the meal was over, and never allowed me to help her with the dishes.

Whether it was in the morning, while we all strolled under the cherry trees after breakfast, or in the evening around the table, I always had a sense of Hugo sliding an arm through mine and steering me away from Rennie. He talked and smiled on and on, like a fortune-teller palming the cards under his patter. I was often reminded of the day he had displayed his trophies and made binocular-eyes at my windows, but I no longer bothered to imagine hot tickling passion in the dry centre of a wheat field. Sometimes, as I lay awake listening to the breath whistle in and out of Rennie's nostrils, I wondered how it would be to let Hugo take me to hear that nightingale. But in the morning, watching him wink *good morning* at me, I remembered all his teasing games. *Here Louise, sit by me,* he would say, patting a chair and smiling invitingly, and I would shuffle into the chair and knock over a cup. *Did you sleep well?* he would ask, and his melting ardent look seemed to be asking a different question. He stared lingeringly, squeezed my fingers as he passed me the salt, and pressed his knee against mine, until I started to respond. As soon as I began to return the pressure on his fingers as I passed him the marmalade, and left my knee next to his, he showed no further interest. He would grab the marmalade without glancing at me, demand more toast, and munch loudly while

67

explaining through a spray of crumbs exactly what happened when Iris was in heat.

This was a house of small mysteries and noises. Sounds echoed strangely off the tiled floors and ran in and out of rooms in unpredictable ways. Voices carried clearly up the stairs from the kitchen, but were lost bouncing from wall to wall in the dining room, so that we all ended up shouting at each other across the table, but understanding little.

The bed Rennie and I slept in together had been Daniel's. He had insisted that we use his bedroom, and now slept directly below us in one of the small and apparently functionless rooms that this house had spawned everywhere. Unlike the tinkling and squeaking one in the mouse-house, this bed was as immovable and silent as a marble tomb. Even so, on the rare occasions when Rennie mounted me, I imagined Daniel listening below. He would hear the way Rennie panted, and his groan when he slumped and lay heavily on top of me. Daniel would not be able to know that Rennie's eyes were tightly shut throughout. But it would probably not be hard to guess that he liked it best when I knelt beside him on the bed and used my hands. *Daniel will hear,* Rennie would say sometimes in the middle of it all. *Daniel will hear us.* He would squeeze his eyes even tighter then, and seem to groan even louder.

10

In the hot night, the lanterns hanging at each stall appeared to drip. The yellow cheeses and the smooth faces behind the counters all sweated discreetly, and smoke from the roast-lamb pit billowed between conversations. When Hugo offered me a chunk of bright-green coconut ice — *very traditional, Louise, at these village festivals* — I wondered whether he really expected me to eat it, or whether it was just a conversation piece. It soon became sticky in its wrapping and I wondered how many more stalls we would have to pass before I could drop it on the ground. I hurried to catch up to Daniel and Rennie, who were striding ahead through the slow-moving crowd, but Hugo took my arm.

— Wait, you'll fancy this.

The merry-go-round was strung with naked light bulbs and in the middle a tiny monkey of a man in tennis shoes shuffled around the revolving platform where he operated the machinery, while tinny music blared from loud-speakers. The gigantic lever he used was polished silver in one spot from all the years of his hand closing around it.

I wondered why the animals on the merry-go-round were swollen pink pigs, not horses. The children riding the pigs were moon-faced with fatigue, and looked ready to slip off the saddles and go to sleep on the floor among the jabbing trotters. Standing around the fence, grinning parents nodded and waved each time their child came around. One enthusiastic father with a baby over his shoulder was demonstrating how the buck-jumpers did it, and when the baby woke up and dribbled down his back, he handed it to his wife so that he could go on bucking and arching like a hooked fish.

— Go on Louise, Hugo urged me with a finger in the small of my back. Local colour. You'll love it.

I imagined myself astride one of these ugly pigs, holding the sticky metal bar and waving at Hugo each time I came around. I would quickly get sick of the slippery plastic between my legs and of Hugo's smile, which would remind me that he had refused at the last moment to join in the joke and had swung off the wheel as it started to turn, making the monkey-man shout angrily.

Hugo slid an arm around my waist.

— Did you know that when babies are born, their genitals are swollen from their mother's hormones?

I took a step out of his arm. I was growing weary of Hugo, and was uneasy alone with him in the crowd. I could not see Rennie and Daniel anywhere. Hugo followed me and put his arm around me again. Seeing me glance up and down the crowded street, he said:

— Leave them. We'll find them later.

Early in the evening, Viola had walked behind a pyramid of golden cheeses and had not come out again. *Her friends,* Hugo had said, and taken my arm. Something about Daniel's back as it moved steadily further and further away and took Rennie along with it, and something about the insistent pressure of Hugo's hand on my arm, was making me wonder if something had been planned.

An old woman in black suddenly rushed out of a tent as if she had planned an ambush and screeched, pointing dramatically at me.

— She knows your future, Hugo said. Want to know your future?

I shook my head and tried to sidestep the old woman, but she followed me, barring the way.

— Tell her I don't believe in the future, I said, and pushed against the woman's shoulder to make her give way. Under the thin black fabric, her shoulder was as hard and muscular as a man's.

Past the fortune-teller, I was caught against a solid wall of slow-moving families. I was wedged for a moment against a dark little stall and saw a cluster of live ducks huddled there in front of a hoop-la stand.

— *Mi scusi, mi scusi,* I said as I butted against a fat back in flowered cotton. Taking advantage of the moment in which everyone turned to stare at my accent, I pushed past. A long web of dribble from a child in a stroller swung loose and stuck to my bare calf.

I had been looking so hard for Rennie that I hardly recognized him when I finally saw him, laughing as he came out of a stall where ragged black cloth almost hid the words *Casa Visitata Dagli Spettri*. Daniel was just behind him and stopped laughing when he saw me.

— Hope you're having a good time, he said. Reynold and I were scared out of our wits in there.

He glanced at Rennie and they laughed again. I made myself smile and felt my face tighten as I stretched back my lips. Still snickering, Rennie took my arm.

— Having a good time, darling? This haunted house thing was fun.

He shaded his eyes from the lanterns with a hand.

— It was dark in there.

He swallowed a sudden laugh. I smiled again, feeling air on my teeth, and drew him out of the way of a soldier who was being followed by half-a-dozen barefoot shrieking children. As he passed me his lips puckered towards me like a wet flower.

The rifles only shot pellets and were sticky from the

many hands that had held them but Rennie was serious as he fitted one into his shoulder, as if he was about to go after an elephant. A tired woman with moles on her chin stuck white plastic pipes into a revolving machine while Rennie squinted along the barrel and made the cloth over his shoulders buckle.

—*Mille lire,* the woman said without looking at him.

I saw that we had arrived back at the ducks and watched the gypsy who ran the stall kicking listlessly at them when they strayed too close to his feet.

—What takes your fancy? Rennie asked. The machine gun? Or the pink dog?

—Don't know.

I glanced over my shoulder at the cluster of people who had paused to watch the big reddish man who was taking up such a businesslike stance behind the gun. A child wiped its nose with a snuffle and tugged at its father's hand. Without taking his eyes off Rennie, the father slapped the child perfunctorily. When Rennie gave the money to the woman, he became aware of the spectators and handed his jacket to me with a flourish, so that I half-expected a murmur or even a catcall, but the smooth Italian faces watched silently. A boy in a leather jacket nudged his companion and grinned. Rennie rolled up his shirt sleeves before he picked up the gun again.

—I used to be pretty good at this. Might be out of practice though.

The man with the snuffling child called his wife over and I felt the woman staring at me. *Inglesi,* I heard, *Inglesi.* Rennie's face was screwed up as if he expected to be jabbed with a pin, and the group behind him was very still as the white plastic pipes began to revolve. There was a series of quick cracks, and a rattle of pellets hit the metal sheet behind the target. Two of the pipes disappeared from the machine, but the rest continued to revolve. Long after the crowd had shuffled on, Rennie stayed hunched over the gun, still staring along the barrel. *Inglesi,* I heard again, and a laugh.

— Well.

He laid the gun carefully on the counter and turned away. I met the stallkeeper's indifferent stare, hesitating, wanting to say something, but followed Rennie without speaking. In the next stall the ducks suddenly squawked in panic.

— I used to be pretty good, Rennie said. I'm out of practice.

He was taking long strides and I was having difficulty keeping up.

— Marching girls, he said, stopping so suddenly that I bumped into him.

As we watched the ten girls in their makeshift uniforms, Rennie rolled down his sleeves and slipped his jacket back on. Putting his arm around me, he squeezed me close to him. The flushed sweating girl who led the troupe was twirling her baton wildly, and he pulled me further back.

— Looks dangerous, he said. And what about that fatty?

He nudged me and pointed to the fat girl wearing high white boots, who was skipping on hot coals in an effort to get back into step.

— About as impressive as I was back there.

We watched the girl's face become agonizingly red. She was biting her lip so hard it seemed that blood was about to trickle down her chin, but she was still out of step when Rennie said:

— I can't bear it. Let's go.

Daniel and Hugo appeared smoothly on each side of us as though they had been waiting for us all along.

— Having fun?

Hugo's arm was bent through mine, pulling me back.

— Yes, and you?

73

I kept my other arm through Rennie's, so that I was sidling along awkwardly between them, feeling as ungainly as a startled hen. Rennie was drawing ahead and my arm was slipping out of the crook of his elbow when I saw that we were back at the shooting-gallery.

— Haven't done this for years, Daniel said, tossing money to the woman, who was breaking open the rifles so violently that her cheeks shook. She handed Daniel a gun and glanced at Rennie and me, but did not seem to recognize us.

— Now, Daniel said and hit Rennie on the shoulder. You have to decide what you want. You might have fun with that.

He pointed to two swords and a grenade, all of reptilian green rubber, that hung together among the dusty prizes. Without waiting for an answer he put the gun up to his shoulder, hardly seeming to take aim before firing six quick shots, and when I looked at the target I saw six shattered pipe-stems revolving. The woman seemed pleased to give away one of her prizes and there was a glitter of gold in her mouth as she smiled at Daniel.

— *Ancora? Ancora una volta?*

Daniel pushed away the gun she was thrusting at him and flourished one of the swords. It wobbled through the air, quivering like something alive.

— Bit on the flaccid side.

With a phlegmy bark he stabbed at Rennie and the sword folded against his chest. Daniel kept thrusting at him, laughing upward like a question at each jab, until the wrinkles around his eyes shone with tears.

— Here, Louise.

Although I caught the grenade he tossed to me, I nearly dropped it when I felt its tepid fleshy texture. Rennie was jabbing back, grunting each time the blade collapsed.

— *En garde, en garde,* Daniel tried to shout. Laughter

74

was warping his mouth like spasms of vomiting so that each word came out as a honk. Rennie's bright-red tongue was nipped between his front teeth.

From the next stall the gypsy watched us and smoked furtively, hiding the butt behind his hand as he puffed. His loud sports coat had been made for a much bigger man. Each time a burst of pellets hit the metal sheet in the shooting-gallery, the ducks at his feet twitched as if electrocuted and their membraned feet flapped against the dust. Offering a handful of rope rings to me, the gypsy said something in a flat jaded voice that did not seem to expect much.

—Lots of fun.

Hugo was nudging me.

—You circle a peg, you win a duck.

He said something to the gypsy, who shrugged and took a last puff at his cigarette, his eyes blank hollows in the crude light of the bulb overhead. When he tossed the butt into the huddle of ducks, their round eyes blinked quickly but they did not move. I wondered if they had had their wings clipped or had just forgotten about flight.

—Well, let's keep on trying, Hugo said, and took my arm again. Daniel and Rennie had disappeared again, but I saw one of the swords scuffed underfoot, the blade dangling from a slimy-looking thread of rubber. This time I did not try to look for them, but allowed Hugo to take charge. He shouldered his way quickly uphill through the crowd, it seemed towards the real purpose of the evening. I decided that if he wanted to find a dark corner where he could whisper flattery into my ear and jam a hand down the front of my dress, I would let him.

At the top of the hill, the street opened into a large square. Here the booths were further apart and men seemed to be about to push them over as they leaned against the counters and downed another free sample of

Chianti Classico. The lights formed a businesslike moat of brightness around the dark shrubbery in the centre of the square. Hugo called greetings to several stall-owners before pulling me over to one where the name BALDUCCI was spelled out in corks. A middle-aged woman leaned over her counter and kissed Hugo on both cheeks. Her face had the grey papery quality of something incurable.

— *Buona sera, buona sera, buona sera.*

She spoke expansively, as if addressing a small crowd. Hugo gestured at me and when Signora Balducci thrust her palm over the counter, the skin, cool and reptile-smooth, made me conscious of the bones as we shook hands.

— She knows we'll buy well from her, Hugo said, watching Signora Balducci uncork a bottle and pour two glasses of pale wine.

— We can get drunk on her samples if we like.

Glancing around at the other stalls, I noticed I was the only female customer, but at that moment Hugo shook my arm and held the glass of wine under my nose.

— Go on, drink, he said. Why do you keep on looking for them? Think I want to kidnap you?

He laughed so hard that Signora Balducci smiled too, showing dark gaps in her teeth.

— I promise I don't, Hugo said with a solemn look over his wineglass.

He took a mouthful and threw his head back so that for a moment I thought he was going to gargle.

— Go on, it's not poisoned.

Although I held the glass, I still did not drink. Something that Hugo said to Signora Balducci made her exclaim sharply and look at me with shock.

— She promises it's not poisonous, Hugo said, and will be offended if you don't drink.

For a moment my throat constricted on the wine as on

a mealy pill, so that I was unable to swallow, and when it went down in a rush I could feel it branching out coldly into my stomach.

— *Bene.*

Signora Balducci refilled my glass.

— *Parla italiano?* she asked.

— *Poco, poco,* I said as I had once before, then Signora Balducci and I stood in a sustained grinning tableau that could have been captioned *The Language Barrier.*

— *Questo vino è molto buono,* I brought out at last, slowly, and Signora Balducci reached across the counter to slap me on the shoulder. Refilling my glass, she repeated what I had said as though it was a code she had to crack, and as soon as I set my glass down it was again refilled with a dark red wine.

— *Chianti Classico,* Signora Balducci mouthed. *Molto molto buono.*

She pointed to the black rooster on the label, showing fingernails of a bloodless blue. Her interest seemed to flag suddenly and the conversation she started with Hugo did not include me.

I stood fingering the stem of my glass, noticing that each bulb hanging from the stall had a tiny halo. It could have been the wine that was making it difficult for my eyes to adjust to the variations of light, and made me see only a rainbowed after-image of the bulbs when I looked away towards the bushes. At the other end of the counter, Hugo and Signora Balducci seemed tiny and a long way off. Feeling that I had been smiling brightly for weeks on end, I let my face relax and stared at nothing.

Up here, where the fair sounded plinking and puny, another kind of life could be heard. A baby wailed from a shuttered house by the square, and I could imagine the large comfortable mother hurrying to the crib to pick up the child, holding it high in the air and cooing until the tiny red face split into a toothless smile. From a side street, a motorbike popped briskly and crackled away into the distance, and a dog barked boomingly from a basement.

I could still hear the ping of the metal pellets against the target, and the thudding of the merry-go-round music, but the sounds were muffled by distance and wine. Out of the corner of my eye I watched Hugo, whose smooth face had never revealed anything more than it had on that first day, when Iris had barked for so long and the grey van had driven slowly up to the steps. I had taken him by surprise only once, in the hen-house. As he had turned guiltily he had dropped an egg that had spattered his foot and I had seen for the first time his gold molar as he grinned. I had decided now that he was determined not to make sense. He was a random event, like weather or the vagaries of rock formation.

In the bushes in the centre of the square, a stream of liquid pattered against leaves and a moment later a man came out into the light shaking one leg and doing up a zipper. Beneath the noises of the fair and the sounds of domestication nearby—now cutlery was tinkling into a drawer—there was another layer of sound, a continual slight shifting and whispering that might have been a breeze. Below that there must have been the sounds of caterpillars chewing their way along leaves and worms writhing into the soil.

—Louise.

Hugo was shaking my elbow.

—She wants you to try some sacred wine.

For a moment I thought he was saying *secret wine*. It was when the sweet wine first touched my lips that I saw Rennie coming out of the bushes, where the leaves must glisten when the light fell across the drying urine. Daniel was walking so close behind him that for a moment he was hidden by Rennie's body. I choked and sprayed sacred

wine on the counter and Hugo thumped me on the back
and cried:

—Not that bad, is it?

Some of the holy wine was trickling down my chin and
I wiped at it as I put the glass back on the counter and
watched my husband come out from behind the bushes
with his friend. Daniel was whispering something into
Rennie's ear and they were glancing at each other and
laughing intimately. Instead of waving to attract their
attention, I stood staring at the surface of my holy wine,
and at the film floating on the surface. It was invisible
until you looked very closely.

Daniel was the first to notice Signora Balducci's
customers. I broke the film on my wine with a finger and
saw how he turned with a few curt words to Rennie, who
looked around as if following the course of a fly through
the air until Daniel nudged him, nodding towards the stall.

My husband looked at me across the space between us
and I saw that he did not, for the moment, know who
I was. His face was blank: I was just another stranger,
a woman he did not know, leaning against a stall holding
a glass of blood-red wine. I saw a stranger, too: the
stranger was the man I had lain beside, all those nights,
and tried to touch, who had not wanted to touch me
except with closed eyes. This man, coming out of the
bushes arm-in-arm with his friend: this was a man I could
recognize, although it had taken me this long to recognize
my husband as a man who belonged to men, not to
women.

11

Too much wine was being drunk again in the arbour of Daniel's garden, and another night was passing in a stupor. Signora Balducci had sold us many bottles of wine that night of the festival, and it seemed that Daniel was determined we should get through all of them.

Daniel picked up the bottle to pour again, and I watched a delicate shell-like moth flutter over Rennie's empty glass. I watched him raise the filled glass to his lips, waiting for him to spit out a mouthful of drenched grey wings, but he drank calmly and wiped his moustache with the back of his hand.

Above us, the leaves of the arbour stirred in the draughts from the paraffin lamp on the table, and the vines crepitated with small noises. Beyond the circle of light, the invisible garden creaked and ticked and the villa stood beyond the bushes, a tall black square against the sky. Rennie and Daniel did not seem to notice the rustlings and shiftings in the leaves above, where thick old vines twisted snake-like in and out of the trellis, but I glanced up at each sound, uneasy, half-expecting to see glittering eyes among the leaves. When something fell on my shoulder I flinched, brushing it off with a shudder that made my chair tilt on the flagstones. I shifted my weight cautiously on the broken slats of the seat. I would only have to be a little heavier to crash through the rotting wood altogether.

Rennie was flushed in the lamplight and pulled an earlobe until it glowed. Daniel opened and closed the clasp-knife that Hugo had left on the table, and used the tip to gouge old black crumbs out of cracks in the wood. The crumbs flew in the syrupy lamplight and came to rest in another crack.

—Even the earth here speaks the language of the Etruscans.

Daniel was murmuring with his nose inches from Rennie's. Rennie swapped earlobes and nodded, his eyelids drooping but his eyes fixed on Daniel's.

—The clay is marvellous for those porous jars.

Rennie nodded again and took the knife from Daniel to flick a line of impacted crumbs from a long split in the tabletop. Watching the tip's uneven course along the wood, Daniel blinked several times and dabbed a finger on each of the empty wine bottles lined up on the edge of the table, beating time to inaudible music. The dark hair that was usually combed neatly across his forehead had become tousled and fell down over his eyebrows, hiding his expression.

—They had the first grapes and the first wine, he said very clearly, watching Rennie. These very grapes — he dabbed at a bottle too hard and it rolled to the edge of the table before he brought his hand down on it — we're drinking the original, really. It's said to possess something or other . . . special.

He trailed into silence and rolled the bottle backwards and forwards as if trying to flatten it. I turned to where I thought east might be, wondering if that was the first streak of dawn I could see, or just pale clouds. The bottle made it over the edge of the table and Rennie and Daniel grabbed for it at the same moment. They panted over it together, Daniel's hand covering Rennie's on the neck of the bottle.

I was so tired now that I would have liked to have left my broken chair and made my way to our tomb-like bed.

Rennie and I had not shared that bed since the night of the wine festival, because he and Daniel stayed each night in the arbour until dawn, drinking and mumbling together, and there came a time each night when I left them there together. The sun was always well up when Rennie came in, smelling of wine and sweat, and fell into the bed beside me, and I did not want to lie there beside him as he snored. I preferred to leave him there, and find a patch of morning sun to lie in, trying to think of nothing but my deepening tan.

There were nights, though, when the wine sang along my veins after a few glasses, and if I had been quite sure of the way through the halls and echoing rooms of the house, I might have been tempted to find the bed where Hugo slept among his trophies.

Tonight he had left the arbour hours ago with a great show of yawning and blinking. I had ignored all his winks and enquiring looks at me as he announced that he was ready for bed. Now I watched Daniel's finger as it made designs in a patch of spilt wine as if spelling out a code. At dinner, Daniel had insisted that we must sample each of the five different wines we'd bought at the wine festival.

—Got to make sure we weren't diddled, he kept explaining as he opened bottle after bottle. That Balducci woman's not to be trusted.

I had tried to stop him when he wanted to fill my glass for the eighth time, but he had prised my fingers off the top of the glass and cried:

—Don't stop now, Louise!

It was the same wine that I had drunk too much of, leaning against Signora Balducci's stall and thinking about my husband, and I had spent the next day with a hangover. But Daniel seemed determined to make me drink too much again, and be reduced to a daze of wine in which anything seemed possible.

—Louise, I think you have the broken chair.

Daniel was flushed in the lamplight and his eyes glittered with the wine, but his voice was as calm as if he was only pretending to be drunk. Next to him, sprawling along the table, Rennie was supporting his head on his hand, his eyelids drooping. A line of black crumbs lay beside a cleaned-out crack and was scattered when his hand slipped off his cheekbone and fell across them. Daniel's movements, as he steadied Rennie's lolling head and slipped an arm around him, were so smooth that he could have been practising them for days. I wondered if Rennie's cheek was as hot against Daniel's palm as it looked.

—Steady now.

Rennie looked up from the table, the smooth wet skin inside his mouth shining as he smiled vaguely. Like a snarling dog's, his lips drew back over his teeth and his eyes tightened into their sockets. When the grimace opened into a yawn laced with strands of spittle, Daniel said:

—You look tired, Louise.

Nodding, Rennie looked at me with eyes suffused and teary from his yawn.

I was watching two gnats wrestle on the table, rolling over and over together, becoming wedged in a crack for a moment and pulling free. Rennie watched them too, his eyes dark and unblinking. He looked at me and smiled.

—I think they're in love.

His smile faded as he continued to watch the wrestling gnats, but I saw a corner of lip caught on a tooth, so that he appeared to be sneering until he ran his tongue over his lips and the sneer vanished.

I felt my pupils expand and contract in an astonished way as I blinked at the lamp filling the arbour with yellow light. I was still astonished, but now I was only astonished

83

that I had lived for so long in a dream, without seeing the truth that had always been there to see. The old wood of the chair creaked under me as I leaned forward, holding the edge of the table to steady myself, feeling the wood crumble under my fingers. Staring at the dark cracks in the table, I followed a series of images of Daniel and Rennie together, sprawled on the Turkish rugs after their run, drinking from each other's glasses, examining each other's thighs, comparing the hair. A long sliver of rotten wood came away from the edge of the table and I brushed the crumbs off my fingers.

When I met Daniel's eyes again he seemed to be nodding at me, but it could have been just the hot pulsing air above the lamp that made his image waver. With Daniel's arm still around him, Rennie was sitting as if waiting for something. I stood up feeling the crown of my head brush the leaves.

— Goodnight, you two.

My voice sounded unfamiliar, as if I had gone deaf. I expected some sign from Rennie that he saw I had finally understood, but he continued to stare into the lamp. When he glanced up, I saw that his eyes were so dazzled he could not see me. My own eyes swam with the blackness of the garden when I stepped out from the arbour. After a moment, making out the dark squatting shapes of bushes and moving forward slowly, my eyes adjusted and I could see the yellow lamplight reach over the grass, illuminating it thinly, but the path in front of me was cast into the shadow of my own body and I had to take each step blindly. I could not remember if there were any obstacles I should avoid.

When I was nearly at the house I glanced back. The two men were as golden as saints in the honeyed light and their heads were close together as they leaned over the table examining a fallen insect. I laid my palm against the front door to push it open and there was a scattering of laughter behind me. The pale band of cloud still lay along the horizon behind the garden, but on the other side of the sky, a glow behind the hills like a distant explosion indicated where the sun was about to rise.

12

The four of us drove to the hot springs in Rennie's car with Daniel at the wheel. *Always wanted to drive something sporty,* he'd announced. Hugo left before us, in the van.

— And the monastery afterwards, Daniel said. First the ritual ablution, then sanctification.

He crunched into first gear.

— Oops. And of course the famous frescoes.

Rennie said nothing, but made a great show of fastening his seat belt.

In the back of the car, I felt that I had less than my share of the seat. On my right, the basket of lunch was making a wicker-patterned indentation in my side, and on my left, Viola seemed to be cramming closer to me than necessary. I caught wafts of sandalwood when she shifted in the seat, and the long scarf she was wearing snapped like a flag in the gusts from the open window, smarting across my cheek. *Sorry.* Viola smiled so warmly at me that she seemed to be accepting an apology rather than giving one, and squeezed the long ends of the scarf deep between her thighs.

Daniel drove flamboyantly along the narrow lanes, using the horn often as if we were rushing to hospital with a woman in labour sweating along the back seat. He shifted gears constantly as he drove so that he rocked in the seat like an organist, and kept up a conversation with Rennie, tossing remarks to him and studying his face for a reaction. In the end I wanted to tap the top of his neat round head and call out *eyes on the road please.*

It had taken us all a long time to get ready to leave. Viola remembered at the last moment that Iris had to be fed, and then she insisted on winding every one of the twenty-four clocks. Then there had been a flurry around the car as everyone tried to decide where they should sit.

—Reynold, I'll need you beside me in case I want to use one of these mysterious knobs, Daniel finally said.

I hoped that he would not fall asleep at the wheel and send us careering off the road. I had only had a few hours' sleep after leaving the men in the arbour, and wondered whether they had slept at all. Rennie had not come to our bedroom by the time I had got up, and he had said *good morning* over breakfast as vaguely as if he could barely remember who I was. I'd exchanged only a few words with him as we all got ready to leave. *Sleep well?* he'd asked. *Yes yes, everything's fine,* I'd said eagerly, trying to convey more in my tone than a good night's sleep, but he had turned to answer a question of Daniel's and had not seemed to hear me. Now his eyes had the fixed stare of someone about to curl up and snore, and he seldom replied to Daniel's chatter. I began by leaning forward to hear what they were saying, but I found that the roaring of the engine made it necessary to watch each mouth as it spoke. After a while I felt like someone at a tennis-match, idiotically swivelling my head between the two men. Now I sat in silence beside Viola, feeling the gusts from the window cracklingly dry as we sped past fields of dun wheat, and dank when we rushed through a wood. At one point, speeding between high dusty hedges, the car suddenly filled with a cloying fragrance as if heaped carnations sweated in the sun behind the hedge.

—Smells like a funeral, Viola said, and I glanced at her with the polite baring of teeth I was in the habit of using with her. I felt my snarling smile fade when she met my eyes insistently, as if trying to say something by telepathy, and I glanced away, embarrassed, in time to see a man in white pyjamas carry a briefcase into a ruined cottage. Viola was still watching me. Wondering if this was some kind of test or contest, I stared without blinking into her eyes, and saw a tiny sharp reflection of myself in their depths. When I turned my head I saw the tiny reflected head move too.

Finally it was I who lost and blinked first.

—Dry eyeballs, I said with a laugh that was a note or two higher than I intended.

Viola nodded, still staring, and moved closer so that I had to resist the impulse to retreat over the basket of lunch. I noticed a tiny pink scar like a feather just above her lip.

—I can see myself, twice in fact, she said.

Viola was so close to me that I wanted to push her huge face away.

—If you got close enough you could see yourself in the reflection of your own eyes, she said. I felt each word as a separate puff of air against my mouth. I strained to see the tiny pinholes of my own eyes reflected in Viola's, and was about to point out that the reflection became darker and fuzzier the closer you got, when she leaned back.

—Sort of like drinking your own bathwater. Vain.

There was such disgust in her voice that I turned away quickly to stare out of the window, feeling my eyes uncrimp from peering so closely. I felt I had been lured into yet another trap designed to make me look foolish, the dimwitted though lovely wife of the man her father was seducing. I watched hard as some kind of large crawling machine in a field deposited a round bale of hay like a fat turd. I tried not to cry. *All the bloody time cat and mouse,* I thought. *These people are vile.* The car sped past a crossroad where two women sat back-to-back on a milestone, both holding baskets on their laps and staring in opposite directions down the road.

— Lovers' tiff do you think?

I found that Viola's hand was on my knee and could not work out straight away what her words meant.

— Those beauties, she explained, jerking her thumb over her shoulder.

I nodded and looked out the window again. I was afraid that Viola would see the glassiness of my eyes and say something that would make the men in the front turn around so that they would all be staring at me and here, in this hot car with the lunch-basket hurting my ribs, I would bawl and bawl.

— Look.

Viola leaned across my lap to point. A man in a tree sawed at a branch that was about to fall on the head of another man stooping below, while the pointing finger and o-mouthed warning of the fat woman in the white apron was going to come too late. I heard Viola snort and myself guffaw. A tear squeezed out onto my cheek and as I wiped it away Viola's hand brushed my shoulder and dropped onto my thigh. *Do not pity me,* I wanted to say, and wanted to brush away her hand. *My husband has his dapper seducer and you have your teasing brother, who might or might not be your lover. But I will not have you pitying me for being lovely but alone.*

— Nearly there, Daniel announced over his shoulder, and I assumed that the valley of the hot springs was on the other side of the ridge we were now climbing. The engine brayed on the steep corners and I hoped we would make it to the springs before the undefined queasiness in my stomach clarified itself as a desire to be sick. Viola's hand, still on my leg, became heavier and hotter with each

89

hairpin bend. Every time, Daniel waited until the last moment before quickly spinning the wheel, and once or twice the back wheels bit into the gravel as he took us too close to the edge. At each bend, I tried not to look down into the valley, where the road we had already travelled was thread-like from this height. I looked up towards where the pale stone walls of the monastery on the crest of the ridge were sometimes visible between the trees. When the car pivoted around on a corner, I shut my eyes.

On one especially nauseous corner, Viola nudged me and pointed out the window at a box on a stand, peaked like a pigeon-roost. I did not want to have to ask *What is it?* in case I was sick, but I saw now that there was one of these boxes at almost every twist in the road. Some had been rusted by years of mountain weather or stood askew, while others gleamed with fresh paint. A small truck was stopped in front of a shiny white one and a man in workman's blue was genuflecting and swinging a rosary. I stared down over the next bend at the boulders scattered across the slope. It would be a long way down and a violent landing.

We had almost reached the monastery at the top of the ridge when the road widened and became the main square of a village, where squealing children threw sticks at each other and a flock of geese hissed at the car. Daniel turned off the square into a narrow street that ran past the back of a few houses into scrub, and then stopped and switched off the motor. I wondered what had gone wrong. Dry bushes crowded in towards the car on all sides and the track did not seem to go any further. The silence roared hugely in my ears and I wondered what came next.

—We'll have to improvise dressing-rooms, Daniel announced, his voice very loud and hearty in the quiet. We all unfolded ourselves from the car and I saw that the track continued as a narrow footpath and that the sound of rushing water was not just in my head. A few yards along the track a stream bubbled through a grassy clearing and Hugo was there, leaning against a tree as if he had been waiting for hours.

—Good trip? he asked, but no one answered. He winked at me, but I did not wink back. I could still feel a hot damp patch on my thigh, where Hugo's sister's hand had lain for so long.

This busy stream was evidently the hot springs, even though it seemed much too small to bathe in. The water emerged from a dense tangle of bushes a little way upstream and disappeared downstream over a ledge of rock. In the space of open water there was room for a couple of bodies, but there were no steps and no marble cubicles, and nowhere to make a wish.

—Girls, why don't you go over there, and we'll go behind these bushes.

With one hand Daniel gestured with his towel, and with the other he steered Rennie towards the bushes. Rennie was glancing from the smooth walls of the monastery down to the stream and back again as though taking measurements. I decided to move over towards him and tell him there was no need for this pantomine of interested innocence. *I know,* I would say. *I know and it's okay.* Perhaps I would even be able to touch him and tell him that I wanted nothing from him. Perhaps I could even tell him I was glad that the failure was not my own. But as I began to move over towards him, Viola gripped my wrist and pulled me away.

—Come on, she said, and I found myself following her across the stream without having even caught Rennie's eye. As I pushed into the bushes, I wondered if the three men were turning to each other with winks and smiles.

The noise of branches being pushed back seemed huge,

and when I stopped in a clearing to wonder where Viola had gone, the silence soughed back against my eardrums. Thin yellow sunlight flowed down the hill like smoke, carrying the shrieks of children with it. I had the feeling that if I turned back to the stream there might be no one there. It was possible that the whole world, and all the complexities of this summer, existed only in my imagination. While I stood listening, the shrilling of the children stopped as suddenly as if a sack had been flung over them, and into a dense pulsing silence Hugo stepped from behind a bush, naked except for a straw hat, his penis erect. He was not at all embarrassed. Dark hair grew up thickly from his genitals and branched over his chest like seaweed and each nipple was ringed with dark hair. His teeth glittered on a smile, but the rest of his face was in shadow.

 —Louise. Well well.

I tried to see his eyes under the brim of the hat. It was easy to imagine taking those few steps towards him that would make us collapse together on the ground. The dry grass would crackle like fire under us and it would not take long for the sun to scorch our naked backs. As I moved to take that first step, Hugo spoke.

 —I mistook you for my sister, he said. I hope I didn't startle you.

In the shadow of his hat his teeth were very white as he walked past me and pushed into the bushes. He seemed to know exactly where he was going.

I stood in the sunny clearing and watched the grass spring back up where he had stepped on it. A bird whistled nearby and there was a smell of shit. Since Hugo had passed across the clearing the silence had begun to fill again, but although I could hear a murmured conversation from somewhere I could not tell whose voices I was hearing. From the direction of the stream there was a splashing noise like metal shavings being tossed from hand to hand, and the reedy cries of the children had started again. I stared at the back of my hand before turning it over. The lines on the palm were as purple as if my blood was coagulating. Clenching and unclenching my hand, I tried to remind myself that the horn-shaped scar on my knuckle was from where I had slipped off my father's roof twelve years ago. The blood began to pound in my head and I forgot to breathe. I stood in that hot and smelly clearing for a long time with the sounds of other people distant in my ears, and could not imagine what might come next.

13

I did not know how much later it was that I changed into my swimsuit and walked back to the stream, making as much noise as I could. I did not want to surprise anyone. Daniel and Rennie were sitting in the narrow stream like passengers in a canoe, Rennie staring downstream at where the water disappeared over the cliff, Daniel close behind him with his chin on Rennie's shoulder. The water that bubbled around them was green against their pale skins.

— Lots of room, Louise. Come on in.

Daniel shifted downstream so that he was jammed even more tightly against Rennie's back, and gestured behind him. I smiled to show I had nothing against the idea, but sat on the bank beside Rennie, paddling my feet in the water and wondering if there was anything left to say to these people.

The water was exactly the temperature of skin, sliding over my feet like a surreptitious caress. When I lifted a foot up, I saw that the tepid water had turned it pink, and wisps of warm air floated around my face. There was some kind of sharp odour, like sulphur or hot metal, or the ammonia smell of a sloughed-off snakeskin left to crumble beside a rock.

— Come on in, darling.

Rennie spoke lazily, making an effort to sit up straighter against Daniel's chest. There was a line as sharp as a scar across his ribs where the skin had turned pink in the warm water. Daniel stared past Rennie's ear at me and when he brushed away a curl of hair clinging to his cheek I was not sure whether it was his own or a strand of Rennie's.

An airless lassitude was soaking up from my feet into the rest of my body so that I felt I might melt over sideways at any moment, like a candle left too close to the fire. A bird with black and grey bandings like a lizard pecked at the ground beside a rock, and above it the wind shook the dry leaves of a tree with a blazing noise.

—My feet are sleepy, I said.

I could see that Rennie was too languid to speak. He smiled and nodded slowly into the distance, while under his foot a stone dislodged a frill of black slime that twisted like a swimming snake as it was sucked downstream. Watching the fronds of his fingers waving in the current, I sometimes counted six fingers, sometimes only four. If he had relaxed much more he would have flowed down the stream and over the lip of the cliff like thick batter from a spoon. When I looked directly at the place where the stream fell into the valley, I could see only the swaying top of a bush that was lodged in a crack somewhere below, but if I looked away I could see out of the corner of my eye the steam rising from the waterfall and floating away in the air.

It was starting to seem impossible for any of us ever to move again, when Viola came out of the bushes in a red swimsuit. Hugo was beside her in brief blue trunks and jumped into the water behind his father, exclaiming at the smell of the water and the way the bubbles crisped against his skin. Viola sat on the bank opposite me as if she wanted to keep the arrangement of bodies symmetrical. Leaning back on her hands, she tilted her face up to the sky, and revealed a fresh red mark, the size and shape of a slice of zucchini, on the side of her neck.

—This isn't good enough, girls!

With a tearing pop like a cork out of a bottle, Daniel prised himself out of the stream and stood up, stepping neatly sideways and gesturing at the space of turbulent water he had left between Hugo and Rennie. Water ran down his legs and formed a puddle around his feet. A bell began tolling urgently from behind the blank monastery wall.

—Ask not for whom it tolls, Daniel said.

He tried to grin but could not stop himself glancing nervously up the hill behind him, and stepped quickly back into the stream after a moment, sitting down with a splash. The instant his chin touched Rennie's shoulder, the dull clanging stopped. In the silence the water bubbled inanely, like a conversation.

—Looks as though they want me to stay here.

Daniel crouched further over Rennie so that his pale back was exposed to the sky.

—There'd be worse places, I said.

Daniel looked at me and nodded hard.

—Yes, yes indeed Louise. Yes indeed.

—What?

Rennie had raised his head from his study of the pebbles on the stream-bed so quickly that Daniel had to jerk back to avoid being hit on the nose. Behind him Hugo retracted his head like a tortoise.

—What did you say?

Winking at me over Rennie's shoulder, Daniel said:

—Just about that bell. Matins or vespers or something.

Rennie stared at me, but I smiled blandly at his damp upturned face. He knew something more had been said, but I was in the mood for having a secret or two of my own. Viola beat her feet up and down on the water, making him cringe from the spray, and when he sighed *please!* she stopped splashing and balanced her soles flat on the surface of the water. She looked as if she was about to try walking on it, but when she stood up it was on the grass.

—Look at these men, she said. Weak as kittens.

She pulled at the edge of the red swimsuit where it had worked up into her crotch and exposed a curve of untanned skin.

—Come on, Louise.

With her hands on her red hips and her legs planted apart, she stared at me challengingly. I did not ask *come where?* but stood up and took the one long stride across the stream. I could not imagine what might happen next, but felt the men sitting watching us like three monkeys. Viola shouted something that sounded like *Olé,* and I caught a glimpse of the bright-pink soles of her feet as she ran.

As the first bush came between me and the stream, the sound of the water vanished as completely as if a door had been closed. Heat hummed between the bushes and the bird was still whistling overhead. I could only see a few feet ahead, and stood listening for a sound that might tell me where Viola had gone. The smell of shit filled the air again, a loud fly zoomed past me, leaving silence behind it, and a twig settled into a tuft of grass with a sound like glass breaking. A set of vague openings like rough doorways between the bushes drew me on, further and further up the hill, away from the stream. The smooth pale walls of the monastery high above were as unstained as if they had been built the day before, and the sky behind them was a blank uninflected blue.

A din of bells suddenly clashed out from behind those walls and a leafy branch slapped my face like a hand. The bells crashed together in the air in a menacing clamour that seemed to want to pin me to the spot. When I saw a flash of red in the bushes up ahead, I crept towards it.

Viola was crouching on the edge of a grassy bank, staring down. She did not look around as I squatted beside her, but pointed slowly, as if not to puncture the air, at the monk lying below us. His legs in clumsy boots were wide apart under his robe and he stared up towards the sound of the bells as if seeing a vision. His hands groped out and wandered down the front of his robe, fumbling at the coarse cloth. Now I could see the way his eyes stared and bulged. His face was tilted up towards the bells as if towards a sun, while he pulled away at the clothing over his crotch.

Viola shifted closer to me and I could feel her thigh warm against my own, trembling from the strain of squatting. A red bug climbed up her toe and slithered across the broad nail before embracing a grass stem. When Viola leaned in to whisper, I could only hear a great rush of close air in my ear.

— What?

She picked up a twig and drew the words TRU LUV on the dust between her feet, laughing silently, her eyes squeezed into two slits. Her face was so twisted with laughter she could not speak, but she nudged me and pointed at where the words she had written were being washed away by a pale-yellow stream that dripped from the crotch of the red swimsuit and steamed up between her thighs. The ground was so dry that it could not absorb the yellow liquid, which spread smoothly in a pool between Viola's feet and sent an exploring finger down the slope. I watched as it slid between grass-stems, bearing a load of tiny bits of twig and leaf, and drawing a crooked line down the hill towards the monk's head. His hand was pumping now among the folds of fabric, and a strand of shining saliva lapped from his mouth. Trickling silently between pebbles and grass, the dusty urine would reach him at any moment.

—Quick.

I wanted to stay and watch, but Viola grabbed my wrist and began to run back down the hill. It would take the monk a while to work out what had happened, then he would bound heavily after us, flattening the grass with his thick boots, and when he caught us his loose wet mouth would shout incoherently and spray spittle at each word.

As the slope tilted suddenly into the valley, Viola let go of my wrist and leapt down ahead of me. We tore through the bushes, racing faster and faster ahead of gravity. Staggering and clutching at a branchful of leaves, I felt my palm burn as my speed ripped the branch out of my hand and under the swimsuit my breasts jarred. Between the bushes further down, Viola's red swimsuit flickered like a tongue. I heard myself panting with abandon. I felt like a parachutist tumbling head-first into space, finally free of the terror of falling.

I burst through a curtain of branches into a clearing where Viola lay spreadeagled on dead leaves. The sun had long since left these trees, and gooseflesh prickled my arms. Here the silence had the smothering quality of a padded cell so that it was hard not to whisper.

—Fun, huh?

Viola's voice was raspy. Her hair stood awry and full of twigs around her flushed face and the shine was still sticky on the inside of her thighs. Lying down next to her on the leaves, I could feel the sweat cool on my skin, and wished I was wearing more. Down here the shadows were dank and the leaves stuck to my back like leeches. When I glanced back up the hill, the bushes seemed to be locked together behind us.

—Why'd we come here?

Viola was leaning on an elbow watching my face for an answer. I licked my lips and had begun a word when Viola yelped:

— That monk!

The chilling silence of the clearing rolled in behind her words. She moved closer to me until we were lying side by side like a couple in a narrow bed, the skin of our legs clammy against each other and the cloth of our swimsuits grating together at the hips.

— Look.

Viola jerked up as though she had spotted an intruder, pointing across the clearing. A leaf sticking to her arm looked like a wound. I crawled on all fours across to a rounded boulder with bleached moss growing all over it, and was about to touch it, wondering what the thick rank smell was, when I saw the maggots crawling among the matted fleece, and the bleached curve of a rib-bone. Viola grunted.

— I want to be cremated, she said loudly. Put me in a jar. Scatter me somewhere.

She crawled quickly back to the middle of the clearing and sat hugging her knees.

— Cheery down here, isn't it?

Her attempt not to whisper gave her voice a reedy breathiness. I cupped my palm over a ball of moss that glowed violently green where a thread of sunlight lay across it. On the other side of the clearing, a dead tree had fallen and bleached with the years, still holding rocks in the death-grip of its roots. Viola seemed oppressed as I was by this sombre place, and was trying to make herself as small as possible. When our eyes met I thought she was about to speak, but she jumped up, yelled something, and plunged into the trees.

I followed her through a thicket where the sun had never touched the earth, and arrived at the waterfall I had watched from above. From down here the water unwound endlessly as if from a hole in the sky. At the top, the water was funnelled out through a rounded black groove and seemed not to be moving until it smashed on the rocks below with a continual angry splintering. As we stood looking up we might have been waiting for the three men to come sliding over the edge. After that moment of ecstasy, when the hand of the water seized you, there would be no turning back.

—People go over these in barrels, don't they? Viola said. Would you?

I shook my head, watching a stick as it was swept over the rim of the falls and down the face of the water. Although I watched for a long time after it had disappeared into the spume at the base of the rocks, I did not see it float back up.

—Someone went over, Viola said.

I picked my way over the rocks to the bent and rusted box on the stand and looked inside. I had wondered what was inside the shrines, assuming something cheaply sumptuous. I had expected the picture of the Virgin, so fogged that it was almost black, but not the broken blue teacup, the empty shampoo bottle, or the tiny skeleton, still stuck with a few feathers. The box was flaking with dark rust inside and smelled powerfully of mould.

Viola was glancing around uneasily. The constant hiss and boom of the falls covered every other sound, so we would not have heard footsteps, and bushes stirred and tossed in the draughts from the falling water. I kept thinking I could see stealthy shapes moving among the trees or hear someone calling.

—A bit spooky.

Viola's voice was a strained whisper, her face green in the shade. A bird trilled from a branch above.

—I think I'm scared.

Her wail of terror was only partly a joke, and she seemed suddenly shorter as she stumbled on nothing, flinging her arms around me like someone drowning so

101

we staggered together on the rocks. The roar of the water applauded and urged us on. Watching my tiny reflection in Viola's eyes, I said:

—Do you trust me?

Viola took my hand and closed her eyes.

—With my life.

I began to pick my way among the rocks away from the falls, feeling Viola stumbling blindly behind me and clinging to my hand. I felt now as though I might spread wings and slowly ascend past the waterfall, or break into a soaring aria, and I held Viola's trusting hand more firmly. Her face was distorted from the effort of keeping her eyes closed and her mouth was set in a rigid grimace of dread. Her shoulders were hunched as though she expected to be hit and her free hand flailed out in front of her. I dragged her along more quickly as the going became more difficult, and although she kept her eyes tightly shut, her mouth gaped wider and wider as if she was opening an eye in the back of her throat. When I stopped she turned her face this way and that like a receptive ear. I squeezed my own eyes shut for a moment, seeing rainbows and bright dizzying dots. When you could not see, it was even hard to tell which way was up. It was all a matter of assumption.

On the other side of the clearing we had stopped in, I saw the dead sheep and realized that I had led Viola in a circle, that the trees and bushes were all alike and every clearing like all the others. Either that, or the hillside was dotted with dozens of rotting sheep.

—Give me your other hand, I said, and Viola held out her palm trustingly. I led her over to the sheep and pulled her fingers down until they brushed the patch of virulent green moss next to the sheep.

—Guess.

Viola bent down blindly and nearly hit her head on a tree-trunk.

—It's that moss.

She was whispering as if it was difficult to speak and feel at the same time.

—Think it's moss?

Viola's hand stopped in mid-air and I noticed that her nails were bitten down to the quicks.

—Then what is it?

I had to fight a grin that was making my words shapeless as I said:

—Remember that sheep?

Viola made a noise like spitting and snatched her hand away. Her eyes, as she blinked in disbelief at the sharp green moss, were tear-rimmed from having been so tightly clenched. She was no longer beautiful and serene, but dishevelled, harassed, afraid. I stopped wanting to laugh and stared at a strand of dead grass that lay twisted between my toes. What I had done did not seem funny any more. I took a deep breath and was opening my mouth to say, *Listen, I'm sorry,* when Viola jabbed me hard under the ribs. I screamed before I realized that I was being tickled, not attacked. For the first few moments I was able to stay calm and knock away Viola's hands, but she seemed to have dozens of fingers.

—No, stop, I began to wheeze from a rubbery mouth. Please.

Viola's face was so close to mine that it was huge and misshapen.

—Are you sorry? she kept saying. Are you sorry?

I could not shape the word *yes,* but doubled over holding my stomach and had a moment's image of Hugo tickling a six-year-old Viola until she wet her pants. It took all my strength to bring my tongue to the roof of my mouth.

—Ssss, I hissed weakly, and Viola let me go.

As we stared at each other, my panting was very loud

and the bird was still whistling calmly somewhere. We were beginning to grin at each other when we heard distant horn-like wails that made Viola's face screw up.

— Better go back.

One of the cries was my own name, distorted by distance into a kind of mooing. The shouting stopped when Viola produced a piercing whistle with two fingers in her mouth.

When I pushed through the last branches I was sweating from the climb past the waterfall and felt leaves and insects sticking to me. I knew that if anyone said anything to me, I would want to slap them. Viola and I did not look at each other, but could hear each other panting.

The men were all dressed and waiting. Daniel's face was cheese-yellow after his soak and Rennie was as pink as a prawn. Only Hugo had not unravelled completely in the water and still had enough muscles left in his face to smile at us. Viola smiled back as indifferently as a madonna but I could see where the tears had dried on her cheeks and could make out the sticky patch where the urine still glistened on her leg. The men would not have noticed, even Hugo noticed nothing, but I knew where to look, and had been there with her.

14

At first it looked as if the only way in to the monastery was by balloon. There seemed to be no opening in the smooth yellow walls until at the very last turn in the road the entrance slyly revealed itself, a drawbridge that crossed a dry moat and led to a gateway. Daniel drove very slowly as he approached the bridge and I could see that an error of only a few inches would be enough to send us over into the brick-lined moat. The bridge tinkled and clattered under the car as each worn bolt strained to hold the slats together, and then we plunged into the darkness of a tunnel where the roar of the engine beat back from the walls. When we stopped in bright sunlight on the other side, my eyes winced from the glare.

The sunlight seemed different here, as if it had been passed through a screen that gave it the thin quality of artificial light. The scene that lay under this pale light had the expectant and false look of a tableau. Loud yellow daisies dotted a patch of very green lawn, and ivy crept from window to window along the low stone buildings. Monks strolled so slowly they seemed to be painted on to the background, their long brown robes drifting against the ground. One ancient monk walked along stooped over a book, and when his hem caught on a twig and fanned out behind him he did not seem to notice.

Daniel spoke in quick Italian to the gatekeeper and thanked him profusely for something.

— *Grazie, tante grazie, mille grazie*, he repeated as he slowly released the brake and let the car roll down the curving road into the grounds.

I wanted to ask *Are you sure they know we're women?* A very young monk with a hairless delicate face peered into the car and I blushed, then turned to watch him through the back window, surprised to see Hugo stop the van beside him. Gathering his brown robes in one hand, the monk revealed black pants that had been made for someone shorter as he climbed into the passenger seat. I caught Daniel's eye in the rear-view mirror when I turned around.

— A good friend. For a while Hugo flirted with the idea of joining this community.

He said nothing more, although Rennie said *Really?* in an encouraging way, and when there was no answer, tried again with *Becoming a monk, you mean?* I turned to look out of the back window again but the van's windscreen reflected the sky. Rennie cleared his throat as though trying to rid himself of his unanswered question, and I wondered if Viola had also thought about a vocation. Her body would soon lose its tan under the apron-thing and the smock-thing and all the rest of the drapery, and probably nuns did not play the kinds of games that would make them laugh so hard they wet themselves.

— The monks have lots of fun. The frescoes are quite famous.

The way Viola spoke made the two facts seem connected.

— Frescoes? What frescoes?

Rennie twisted around in his seat.

— Down in the main cloister.

Daniel pointed further down the hill and when Rennie continued to watch his mouth for more information he added:

— We'll see them tomorrow.

Beyond the first lawn there was a low building and

beyond that there was another lawn and another, more impressive building. Outside the first, with its discreet notice, *osteria*, Daniel stopped the car and turned to look at me.

—They're very nice people here.

We all watched a monk swinging the tassle of his rope belt as he stood under a tree.

—Very broad-minded.

With one foot already outside the car, Rennie stared at Daniel. With a relieved sense of clearing myself of some obstacle, I said:

—You think they'd prefer it if Rennie and I didn't share a room here?

Rennie looked from face to face, watching each set of lips as it moved, like a lip-reader having difficulties.

—Exactly.

Daniel gave me a glittering smile.

—Hope you won't mind my stealing him for the night. Of course you'll have Viola.

Viola and Daniel both watched me closely and I felt as exhilarated as someone successfully speaking another language for the first time.

—Fine. Sounds fine with me.

Rennie brought his foot inside the car and looked from Daniel to me and back again.

—You mean they won't let us share a room?

—Certainly not, Daniel said cheerfully.

—And what about Hugo? Rennie asked.

I saw Viola and Daniel exchange a glance.

—Oh, he'll sleep with one of the novices, Viola said after a pause, and I wondered if that was a wink at me that I saw as she met my eye for an instant.

Inside the *osteria*, I practised my Italian trying to understand Daniel's negotiations with the huge bulldog-faced concierge, who was offering us adjacent rooms.

—*Questa per le signore, questa per i signori*, she exclaimed and gestured from one room to the other.

Daniel said something that made her crow in surprise and with a martyred sigh she took out a gigantic bunch of keys from somewhere in her grey dress and led the way to the other end of the corridor. As she walked, her legs seemed to bow outwards under the weight of her body. Outside the room at the far end of the corridor, there was another burst of argumentative Italian. Viola joined in this time and all three shouted at once until a gaunt bald man poked his head out of one of the other rooms and asked querulously in English:

—What's going on? What's all the row?

I stared at him and shrugged rudely as if I did not understand English.

—What's all the fuss? Rennie asked. What's happening?

I looked at his heavy face and the way the frown drew his eyebrows so close together they almost met. When he was irritated, his pale eyelashes seemed to disappear altogether and leave his eyeballs naked.

—Don't mind, do you darling? Sharing a room with her, I mean.

I shook my head, but before I could finally say *Look, don't worry, I know and it's okay*, Daniel approached us with a brilliant smile.

—A much nicer room.

He stood nodding at Rennie and bouncing lightly on his feet.

The room I was sharing with Viola was bare and box-like and in one corner a grey dampstain flaked whitewash onto the floor like dandruff. A wooden crucifix hung above each of the narrow beds, and under a small hand-basin there was a plastic dish like a baby's bath on a stand. Viola saw me looking at it and said:

—A bidet. Or basin.

She laughed.

—For washing cheeks in, anyway.

She bounced up and down a few times on one of the beds, making the springs squeak and the metal frame tap against the wall. She frowned.

—Noisy. Are they both like that?

The other bed screeched along the tiled floor at each bounce.

—Very indiscreet.

A sharp male cough from the next room seemed to agree with her.

At dinner in the guests' gloomy dining hall, Daniel yawned and stretched throughout the meal and spoke several times of *turning in early*. He insisted that everyone must try the liquor the monks made, but did not touch his own glass of the dark liquid.

—Here, Reynold, you'll have to finish mine.

He pushed his glass towards Rennie, whose eyes already seemed to waver in their sockets and who obediently took the liquor and drank steadily. When he had emptied the glass he put it down on the table harder than was necessary. I winced, expecting to see him flinch back with a handful of jagged glass.

Back in the *osteria*, Rennie forgot that he was sharing a room with Daniel, and took my arm as if to go with me into the first room.

—No, no, Reynold. Tonight it's you and me, remember?

The concierge, her face creamed greasily for the night, appeared at a doorway and watched until we had gone to our rooms. Viola stood looking at the two beds. When the concierge's door slammed loudly she flinched.

—I'll take the wall side if that's okay.

Her voice seemed to echo around the bare white room.

There had still been a green glow in the sky as we had left the dining hall, but now the square of the window was so black that it could have been painted on the wall. There were no curtains and the shutters seemed to be locked open. If monks were standing outside, jostling each other to peer in at the signorinas undressing, they would be invisible.

— Bathroom, said Viola, and left.

I lay on the bed nearest the window and looked at the dark stain on the ceiling around the light fixture. Black strands and specks glided over the walls when I looked away from the bulb and I had to stare into the darkness under Viola's bed and blink before I could make sure that there really were spiders hanging above me. They had caught something and were mummifying it in strands of web, but as I watched, the wrapped bundle swung loose. When it fell onto the front of my shirt I flicked in horror at the sticky lump until it flew across the room and landed on Viola's bed. After a moment I picked it up, seeing the blue metallic bulb of a fly underneath sticky grey threads. When it convulsed in my hand, I was revolted and tried to throw it away, but the web stuck to me and finally I had to wipe the clinging lump off onto the blanket.

The spiders were hanging above me without moving. I wondered how many days they had had to draw out web from themselves before they had caught anything, and how many times they had had to sting the fly before it stopped buzzing and lay paralysed, waiting to be bound. I picked the fly up by one sticky leg and tossed it up into the web. The leg broke off, sticking to my finger, and although the fly hit the web, it tore loose and the spiders scuttled away from it.

Viola opened the door as I picked up the fly from the bed. The grey filaments of the web were now melting together and the bulb of the fly had been flattened on one side.

—It fell, I said.

Viola peered at the fly and at the web.

—Maybe it's a present, she said. Pop it in your mouth, go on.

A fleck of toothpaste beside her nose jumped up and down at each movement of her face as she spoke. The fly was sticky on my palm now and I wanted to be rid of it. I held it up towards the spiders as if elevating the Host and then put it carefully on the windowsill.

—Think spiders have good eyesight? I asked.

Viola shrugged and turned her back. I lay on the bed staring up at the halo on the ceiling and listening to her undress. The shirt was unbuttoned, the jeans were unzipped, and the bra snapped against flesh as it was unhooked. When she leapt into bed she made the springs twang. I glanced at her then, thinking that she would be hidden under the bedclothes, but she had pulled the sheet up only as far as her waist and had pushed the pillow under her back so that her breasts were thrust up at the ceiling. Her nipples were long and wrinkled.

—Good for the back, she said without looking at me. Then she turned and winked. There was no doubt this time about the wink.

—I took a shower, she said after a moment. She said nothing more and as the silence extended, I felt her remark was a suggestion or even a kind of demand. I seemed to be enunciating the words too clearly when I finally said:

—Good idea. Think I will too.

Although the *osteria* was so fussy about men and women sharing a bedroom, there was only one bathroom, a large room fully of gloomy wooden cubicles. I glanced into several of these before finding one that was a shower, and quickly washed in the tepid water. While I was towelling myself, I heard slow footsteps that came in and stopped in the middle of the room. I paused in my towelling, wondering if it was Rennie, but there was no further sound. I was about to call out — *Rennie, that you?* — but remembered the irritable Englishman. Or perhaps those heavy footsteps belonged to the grey concierge, and it could turn out that women were not permitted in this bathroom. Perhaps, after all, there was another *bagno* for women somewhere. The door of the cubicle would be slammed back and the woman's voice would shriek in outrage until Daniel appeared in his striped English pyjamas, cracking his knuckles in embarrassment. His voice would fade to a reedy whisper, trying to placate her. Hardly breathing and afraid to straighten up, I crouched over the crumpled towel. I was beginning to quiver from the effort of holding myself like this, when the person in the middle of the room let out the single loud bark of a long-suppressed fart. There was a sigh and the footsteps left the room.

I finished drying myself so quickly that I was still damp when I returned to the bedroom, where Viola seemed to be asleep, although every corner of the room was still exposed in the light of the bare bulb. The spider web hung empty, already looking ragged and abandoned. The spiders had disappeared and the fly was still on the windowsill. After I switched off the light, the dense darkness of a sealed tomb pressed against my eyes and I shuffled cautiously towards the after-image of my bed. In spite of my care, I went astray by a few inches, stubbing my toe on something that hurt, and heard a pulsing sound from Viola's bed. I decided she was laughing again.

— It's not funny, I said, but I was laughing too as I felt my way along the edge of the bed.

Viola did not reply, and as I lay listening to the humming silence it occurred to me that the sound I had heard might have been a sob, not a laugh. I lay stiffly, listening for another sound and trying to think of something to say that Viola would have to answer.

I woke up shivering from a dream of refrigerators and ice floes. The room was still dark but a patch of grey showed where the window was. Cold under the thin blanket, I shifted in the bed and heard a rustle as Viola moved too.

— More blankets anywhere?

Her voice sounded half-awake and cross. I said:
— I'll look.

The corners of the room were painfully square when the light snapped on. The bulb swayed and the shadows of the furniture shifted as if everything had been moving quietly around the room and had just now stopped. The closet with the cracked door held only a scattering of moth-balls and one hanger that swung in a startled way when I opened the door.

— Nothing. I'll look outside.

At each end of the corridor, a dim bulb made the linoleum of the floor gleam with colourless light. The closet near the door was locked with a heavy brass padlock, although the hasp was so flimsy that a tug could have pulled it straight off. At the far corner of the corridor there was another closet and I tiptoed down towards it, the soles of my bare feet making kissing noises on the waxed floor. As I passed the Englishman's room, I heard a single loud cough like a chairman calling a meeting to order. I was moving so slowly down the corridor that when a figure came out of a room a few yards ahead and went into the bathroom, I escaped notice by flattening myself against the wall, and stayed there for a moment before gliding forward again from one foot to the other and steadying myself with a finger against the wall.

At the open doorway of the bathroom I stopped to listen, ready to start walking with large frank steps if anyone came out. I thought the figure I had seen cross the corridor might have been Daniel, but although I could hear a murmuring voice in the bathroom that sounded like his, it spoke more and more softly as I approached the doorway. With my ear pressed against the door-jamb, I could see a section of bathroom wall, the blue paint flaking off and showing the dark bricks beneath. Projected on this wall, two shadows moved together. A stream of liquid began to tinkle, joined after a moment by another stream that made a deeper, more authoritative sound. The two shadows had drawn together and become a shapeless blot on the wall when I heard a rumble of words from Rennie. Someone guffawed and the shadow split so that I could distinguish Daniel's shorter shape from Rennie's bulk.

The mumble of Daniel's voice continued above the liquid noises and his shadow swayed backwards and forwards as if he was rocking on his toes. I began to shudder with cold, tucking my hands into my armpits and covering one foot with the other, but stayed straining to listen until the stream finished in plinking drips. Almost running, I tiptoed quickly back down the corridor. I could feel my lips drawn back into a wild grin.

Viola lay coiled up in the middle of her bed with the blanket doubled over her. When the door closed, she lifted the edge of the blanket and showed a single eye that blinked at the light.

— Got any?

— No.

— Fuck.

The curtain of blanket came down again and she squirmed, trying to burrow into the mattress. I pulled the blanket and sheet from my own bed and spread them over her, and was careful this time to measure the distance from the floor to the bed before I switched off the light. Viola stiffened as I slid into the bed with her but then she sighed and folded herself around me until we were lying front to back like two spoons in a drawer.

— Better?

I imagined someone pressed up against the edge of the window frame, watching the dark hump on the bed heave and stir.

— Mmmmmmmm.

The palms of Viola's hands were as smooth as unstamped coins on my flesh.

15

It was just after dawn when a bell with the cracked flat tone of a sour face tolled for a minute and stopped. I woke up staring at the bright square of the window and a dark cypress branch gesturing across it. Next to me on the pillow was a scribble of dark hair and a pair of eyes that flickered open, stared into mine, and closed again.

—Too damn early.

I wondered what Rennie and Daniel were saying to each other as they woke up. Viola was warm and heavy against me, fast alseep again, and I lay watching how each of my breaths made the hair dance around her ear. She smiled faintly as she slept on, until another cracked bell woke her again, and this time, reluctantly, we uncoiled our bodies from each other and got out of bed.

I was curious to see Rennie transformed, perhaps glowing and vivacious this morning. But each time Viola and I tried to walk along the corridor towards the room he shared with Daniel, the concierge appeared from nowhere and stood in the middle of the corridor staring at us until we changed our minds and returned to our room. She appeared at our door with an armful of dirty sheets which she dropped before stepping laboriously over them into the room, and her movements as she ripped the sheets of Viola's bed were as violent as if she expected to find something incriminating underneath. I guessed that Rennie and Daniel were probably enjoying a long sweaty jog together around the grounds. Either that or they were still in bed.

116

—Breakfast? I asked, and Viola nodded.

We walked in silence towards the dining hall, through a grove of shimmering young trees. I glanced sideways at Viola and saw her smooth sleepy face split into a lewd grin.

—Hugo likes to pretend I'm a boy, she said, and smiled at an old monk who was kicking through the dust with his sandals. *Buon giorno, padre.* So I'm still a virgin, really. Am I?

Leaping into the air she broke off a twigful of leaves and caressed her face with them thoughtfully.

—We probably won't see him this morning, she said and nibbled at a leaf. After his night with the novices. His debauch.

She said the word as primly as if she had just learned it.

The dining hall was almost empty and there was no sign of Rennie or Daniel. Viola and I ate breakfast quickly, turning guiltily towards the door each time it opened. I had reduced a bread roll to damp pellets and was arranging them into hieroglyphics on the tablecloth when Viola said through a yawn:

—Let's go. They can find us.

She led the way down a twisting stone path with a certainty that showed she had been here before. Under the breeze, the saplings fluttered in alarm but further down the hill towards the centre of the grounds the air became still. On the other side of the trees and beyond an expanse of lawn, a sombre prison-like building absorbed sunlight.

—Where are we going?

I could hear the anxiety in my voice.

—Sure we're allowed in here?

Viola said nothing, but left the path and struck off across the springy lawn. I took the longer way around by the path, hurrying when I saw Viola disappear into

117

the blackness of a doorway. The lawn seemed suddenly as empty as if she had never existed. I hurried through the doorway into the chill of the building and was stifled by the darkness.

— Come on.

Viola's voice was impatient and I faltered towards it with outstretched hands. Just as my eyes had begun to adjust so that I could make out another tall door, Viola pushed through it and was gone. Chanting, as thin as the whine of insects, could be heard for a moment before the door swung shut again. I pushed against the sticky patch near the handle, shiny from the touch of hundreds of palms, and found myself in the back of the church where male voices droned on and on as if memorizing a list. In front of a big blue statue the flames of clustered candles all leaned sideways. Cold light fell across wicker prie-dieux and up in the darkness of the vaulted roof, a lamp swaying in the draught glowed blood-red. The monks stood near the altar, only their pale faces and raised hands visible in the dimness. A single kneeling figure was collapsed over a prie-dieu at the front of the church. I thought it looked like the concierge.

Viola beckoned to me from beside a holy water stoup in the shape of a scallop-shell, trailing her fingers in the stoup while I reluctantly joined her, imagining the icy stagnant water and the slime around the edge of the scallop-shell. I was close enough to see the shine on Viola's forehead where she had blessed herself when she flicked a sudden handful of water into my face. The cold greasy drops ran down my cheeks and I exclaimed into a pause in the music. Viola shook a finger at me, hissing *Shhhh*, then walked away down the side of the church towards another door, while I followed, afraid of being left behind but nervous of making any more noise. As we reached the doorway a monk emerged. Viola curtsied but I stood with my head bowed stiffly while the monk sketched a cross in the air between us. I wondered if he could see the spots of water on my face.

Beyond the second door there was another, apparently functionless lobby. I had lost all sense of direction now and felt as though Viola and I were wandering in corkscrew circles.

— Where are we?

Viola hurried on without answering. Beyond the lobby was a series of small dark rooms like saunas lined with planks, then our footsteps echoed sharply as we walked through the monks' refectory. At the far end, a moon-faced novice stared at us, frozen into a still-life as he laid a spoon beside a plate. We left the refectory and I wondered whether he would go on laying the seventy-six spoons in place. Perhaps he would drop the lot and run shouting the alarm that would bring monks out of doorways everywhere to bar our path.

Through the high slit windows, I could now catch glimpses of a patch of blue sky against orange roof-tiles, and a piece of wall with ivy crawling over it. Viola stopped in front of a final massive door and waited for me. Just before she pushed it open she said:

— You look nice when you're scared.

The light in the cloistered courtyard was so intense that everything was bleached of colour, so that the peeling plastered columns and the overgrown dry fountain had the look of someone's fuzzy black-and-white holiday snapshot. The only thing that moved was the drifting seed-fluff from the weeds that sprang out of every crack. I was glad to leave the smell of incense and dark wood, but wondered how I would ever find my way out again.

The frescoes covered two walls of the cloisters. Saints with big yellow halos like cheeses stood clutching staffs and jars, and blank-faced women knelt at their feet with babies. Each scene provided a reason for at least one male figure to wear almost nothing. A handsome beggar clutched at the rags slipping off his hips in one fresco, and in the next a young man with a falcon was pointing to the slit in his cloak that revealed a melon-round bare buttock. A figure that appeared in several scenes was a devil who wore only red tights and a drift of drapery. The saints and the women holding their ham-like babies had the wooden faces of bad actors, but the devil was so real that he looked as if he was about to turn and complain from his small rose-like mouth that he was freezing his balls off.

I felt that I had been staring too closely at the devil's buttocks and bent to read a caption. I was so intent on making out the faded lettering — S. *Bartolomeo in something or other* — that I did not realize that Rennie had been standing beside me for some time. I jerked back and clutched the front of my shirt as he took hold of my elbow.

— Got to talk to you.

He was staring straight in front of him at Satan's red tights as if he and I had never met.

— Tremendous, isn't it?

Daniel was on the other side of me and took my arm as if about to march me into the scene flaking on the wall.

— The monks here are notorious, of course.

His voice rang out cheerily into the courtyard and he moved on to the next fresco. When he was out of earshot Rennie said:

— Got to get away from these things.

He led the way to the centre of the courtyard and sat on the crumbling stone fountain. Glancing around continually, he tore at a tuft of grass clinging to a crack.

— We've got to leave. Straight away.

I wondered whether it was the thick sunlight on the top

of my head that prevented my knowing what he meant. He had torn the grass out of the crack and was cleaning every crumb of dirt away with his fingers as if it was very important to do a thorough job.

—Leave?

I heard my voice, as strident as a bird's call.

Rennie nodded and bent down to blow the last few grains of dirt from the crack.

—We've got to leave.

—You and me, you mean?

—Who else?

He looked at me for the first time. The skin under his eyes was flaccid and although his forehead was beaded with sweat his cheeks were like dough. For a moment I could not remember his name.

—I thought he's what you wanted, I said confusedly.

Rennie's eyes flickered as though I'd struck him in the face and he started to say something, but got up unsteadily. He had taken a few steps towards the cloisters when he bent over quickly as if he had just spotted something valuable on the ground. I heard the tearing sound of a retch. I stood up and saw that Daniel had heard it too and was looking blankly at Rennie, and that Viola stood with both hands around one of the columns, staring. Between them, Hugo was framed in the doorway that led into the monastery, and behind him, a young monk with a wide red mouth blinked at the brightness and craned over Hugo's shoulder to see what was happening. There was not much to see. Rennie retreated away from all of us until his back was against one of the columns. In the oppressive sunlight his face was green and his movements as laboured and angular as a broken machine.

16

Back at the villa, where the rooms of the complicated house seemed to have multiplied in our absence, Rennie continued to whisper to me: *Just get us out of here*. He could not move, and lay on our bed with a wet sock on his forehead, saying over and over: *Get us out of here*, until I understood what he meant. His eyes were glassy and when I took his hand to reassure him, his fingers were cold and damp. I left him in the bedroom, staring at the ceiling, and went down to the kitchen to explain. *Rennie is ill, Rennie is unwell*, I repeated over and over, and in fact he did have the stricken dazed pallor of someone who's just lost an arm in a threshing-machine.

Daniel sat between his children at the kitchen table like a prisoner. When I explained, *We must leave in the morning*, he shifted creakingly in his chair, coughed a few times, and finally said:

— I'm so terribly sorry Rennie's unwell. Terribly sorry.

He coughed again and met my eye for a moment. He seemed to have shrunk since the previous day and could not look at anything for more than an instant, as if everything was too brightly lit. Hugo and Viola seemed unsurprised by all these events. It made me wonder whether something like this happened every summer.

— So you're really going?

Hugo still looked cross, and when I nodded, he got up and stood behind Daniel so that for a moment he seemed about to strangle him, then dropped his hands onto his father's shoulders, pressing his thumbs hard into the flesh.

But when Daniel stretched his head forward to enjoy the massage, Hugo turned and left the room. We could all hear Iris welcoming him outside, and the tinkle of the chain as he released her.

Viola said nothing but her eyes seemed to get larger and darker every moment and I wondered what I would do if those huge eyes began to spill tears. Leaving us to our goodbyes, Daniel left the kitchen. I listened to make sure he was not going upstairs to the room where Rennie lay and heard him go along the passage to his own room. I imagined him lying on his bed staring up at the ceiling, directly below the bed where Rennie was doing the same thing.

I glanced out the window, seeing that the huge setting sun was about to touch the roof of the house opposite, where Rennie and I had spent all those nights. The mice in there would be running through every room again, fearless now that the humans had left, and by now Domenico had probably taken every chair into the barn. The sun shot a last few rays into my eyes before sliding down into the black silhouette of the house. A shred of cloud left behind turned suddenly pink.

—So you're leaving.

Viola must also have been watching the sun, for she spoke with a sigh in the moment of anti-climax after the sun had sunk from sight. I continued to stare at the fading glow along the horizon and wondered who would be the next to walk into that bedroom and see the layer of powdery grit on the pillows. I had waited all those weeks for the decaying beam to collapse and crush what lay beneath it, but now that Rennie had buckled, and every pore on his face gasped for air, I knew I would have to leave with him.

When I was ready with some words to explain, I turned around but Viola was no longer in the room and did not appear again that evening. I cooked soft-boiled eggs for Rennie and myself, noticing that, although everything in Viola's kitchen was as new and spotless as a stage set, the knives were all very blunt. Rennie and I spoke in occasional whispers as we sat swallowing soft egg together upstairs.

— Can we go first thing in the morning? he asked and I nodded yes.

Next day, so early that we left footprints in the dew, we crammed our things into the car. We were nearly ready to go when Daniel and Hugo came to the front door in dressing-gowns and Iris started to bark into the quiet morning, and as we took the last armload down to the car, Viola appeared. For once she was not fully dressed, but wore striped pyjamas like Daniel's and was barefoot. Daniel held out his hand but did not seem surprised when Rennie appeared not to notice it. A bloodstained morsel of cotton wool was stuck to Daniel's jaw. His son had not shaved and his chin scratched against mine as he kissed me several times and squeezed my shoulders. Bending over Iris, Viola was trying to silence the barking, and kept crying *Quiet! Quiet!* while I crouched awkwardly and tried to embrace her. When Iris's wet nose and slavering tongue began to investigate my crotch I stood up, reaching out to touch Viola's hair in a last goodbye, but at that moment Iris pulled against the chain and Viola ducked her head away angrily. No one said goodbye, but Hugo told us to drive carefully.

At the very last moment, as I was settling myself into the car, Viola broke away from the group watching from the steps and ran over the gravel to the car.

— Come back, she whispered, and my hand went to the doorhandle, because I did not want to go, but I did not open the door because I could not stay either. Viola saw me reach for the doorhandle and then think again, and she said:

—Come back any time, I'll be here.

I reached clumsily out the window to touch her cheek, but struck my elbow hard on the windowframe and in the moment that I grimaced, Rennie let in the clutch. We were on our way, and I had not asked where our way was.

As we drove away I turned to wave one last time and Viola tried to wave back, holding Iris, who was barking madly as she had on the first day. I tried to remember how the driveway and the house had looked, and how Viola had looked to me then, when I did not even know what language she spoke, but it was like trying to remember childhood. It seemed to have been someone else who had circled this house looking for signs of life and hoping the barking would not bring the police, and it seemed necessary not to remember the feel of Viola's flesh against my own.

We drove in silence as far as the village where the fair had been held. As we drove slowly up that street, still littered with pieces of paper from the green coconut ice, and turned into the square where we had all drunk too much of Signora Balducci's wine and avoided each other's eyes, Rennie relaxed at last. As if it had been throttling him, he loosened the buckle of his belt and pulled out his shirt-tails. His sigh seemed to suggest that he had been holding his breath for hours.

—Couldn't stand that place another second.

Under the pale skin, blood was flowing again in his face and his eyes moved as quickly as a wary animal's, checking frequently in the rear-view mirror. At the end of a long process of thought he reached over and pressed my hand.

—Thanks darling, you were wonderful.

He appeared to have lost a great deal of weight in the last twenty-four hours. I could clearly see the shape of his jaw and cheekbones as he drove along the endless highway. I watched the lump of muscle on his jaw shift as he drove, as if he was carrying on a conversation behind his clenched teeth.

Wanting to put as much distance as possible between himself and San Giorgio, he delayed stopping for lunch until my stomach was audibly growling. When he drew up at last in front of a *trattoria* we got stiffly out of the car, and I stared down the road the way we had come before following him inside. I was certain that I would recognize the grey van if I saw it. Rennie sat down in the very back of the *trattoria*, where three slow flies circled in the draught and the light was so dim that I lost my fork. Rennie ate voraciously. He had finished the bread even before the main dish was brought, and had to ask for more. The day before, he had refused to join Daniel and his children for a meal and had even refused Viola's coffee, drinking only water from his own bottle.

— I would never have thought it, he said suddenly at the end of lunch, his voice cutting across the noise of the cars on the road outside, each one like a flame blazing up and fading away. He glanced around the gloomy room, watching the flies, then looked quickly at me as though to take me by surprise. I shook my head and touched his fingers. Even his hand as it lay on the stained tablecloth seemed thinner and more fragile, the bones sharper under the skin. He held my hand tightly for a long time and I could feel the clamminess of his palms.

After lunch he drove steadily and in silence for hours. He did not want me to take a turn at the wheel, but when we stopped for petrol he bought a big bottle of mineral water and once in a while he would clear his throat and ask me to pass it to him. The car was so noisy that he had to shout above the engine.

At the beginning of the long drive I tried to distract him with small features of interest in the landscape.

Sometimes we passed something that I remembered from the trip down, when we had become so lost looking for Aretta. For most of the way, though, the only indication that we were still not driving towards Tuscany and our summer in the villa was that it was my arm and not Rennie's that was becoming sunburnt as the day wore on. As we left behind the hills and vineyards of Tuscany there was less and less to say and even the names of the villages became less interesting. We watched the vineyards and olives give way to a grey plain across which fences speared in straight lines as far as the eye could see.

Rennie drove without speaking while I listened to the roar and whistle of the wind around the doorframe. It was very hot in the car and the hair over Rennie's forehead was dark with sweat, but with the window open the noise was deafening. When the windows were closed the car smelled of earthworms and decay.

I still thought it possible that he would change his mind, stop the car, and go back. At the intersection he hesitated instead of taking the road ahead to London, so that the cars behind us started to honk. I leaned forward eagerly—was it possible he would change his mind and return?—but when he grunted and swung the car onto the *Milano* road, I realized that returning to Tuscany was not an option he had considered.

17

The fat woman who ran the *Pensione Dora* took our passports and spent a long time comparing the photographs with the people standing in front of her. At last she commented that I looked more friendly in my photo than I did in life, and that Rennie was *più bello*. Rennie seemed reluctant to leave his passport with her. As we followed her labouring ankles up the stairs he said:

— They want to keep tabs on you wherever you go. Follow every move you make.

— Who?

He was watching his hand slide up the carved banister and did not answer.

That night as we prepared for bed a moth flew into Rennie's ear while he sat on the end of the bed doing his breathing exercises.

— Fucking hell, he shouted, and stamped around the room hitting the side of his head with his palm.

Finally he sat on the bed and looked glumly at me. One side of his face was very red.

— I think it's died in there. I can't feel it moving.

He shook his head sideways until his hair was standing on end.

— Have to sluice it out, he said. Castor oil. We got any?

We had no castor oil, but I quickly dressed again and went out to find a *farmacia*. When I came back the room was thick with a smell of burning horsehair. Rennie woke up coughing, his eyes streaming, and we saw that he had fallen asleep with the bare bulb of the table-lamp beside his ear, and that it had burned a neat hole through the blankets and both sheets. It had only stopped after burning its way a few inches into the mattress, exposing a curve of shiny spring.

— They're attracted to light, he said. So I tried this. Now I'll never know if it came out.

He shuddered and began hitting his head again wearily, and even after we had turned the light out and said *goodnight darling*, and *goodnight darling*, he could not sleep, but tossed and turned. Each time I was almost asleep I was roughly woken by an elbow in the small of my back and a loud whisper:

— Oh sorry darling. Go back to sleep.

Finally I sat up, wide awake, and tried to keep the exasperation out of my voice as I said:

— What's the matter? Can't you sleep?

Rennie groaned and when I repeated the question and touched him on the shoulder, he said:

— There's someone outside.

I sat rigidly in the bed listening so hard that the silence made me dizzy.

— He's been walking up and down all night, Rennie whispered. He comes to the door and stands there. I can hear him.

I turned but could see only a lighter patch of darkness where his face was. I opened my mouth hugely, feeling my eyes widen balefully towards him, and stuck out my tongue. Hearing the tiny liquid noises of my mouth he said *what?* but I did not answer, only slid out of bed and padded across to the door. Careful to make no noise, I laid my hands on the latch and in one movement unlocked the door and pulled it wide open. It gaped onto the grey corridor, which was very dirty under the light of the dim bulb, and quite empty. As I stepped out to look more clearly I imagined how easy it would be to close the door and lock Rennie in. I would be able to get a long way from the *pensione* before his yells would be understood and the door unlocked.

I woke up just after dawn to the sound of someone retching in the courtyard below. In the instant of being first awake I thought myself back in the bedroom at San Giorgio, and Viola somewhere under the same roof. When I remembered that I was alone with Rennie again, far from those brown villas and vineyards, I longed to turn over and sleep again. The bed was empty beside me. Rennie was crouching by the door in his brown nightshirt, munching on something and holding several sheets of typing paper. He appeared to be eating the paper like slices of bread. As I watched he stuck two fingers into his mouth and pulled out a lump of chewed paper which he pressed carefully into the keyhole. He stood up and stared at the door, then came back to bed.

— He was trying to see in, he explained, and I did not ask *who?*

We lay awake for a long time without speaking, watching the walls turn from grey to pink as the sun rose. When Rennie finally spoke, his voice seemed painfully loud.

— Let's find another place tomorrow.

I did not ask *why?* but continued to stare at sunrise on the wall. After a while he said:

— I think we can do better, that's all.

I nodded and felt the bed shake with my movement. There was another silence, then Rennie rolled over abruptly and sat up.

— After all we'll be here quite a while. Might as well be comfortable.

He glanced at me to see if I was going to say anything. When I did not, he spoke loudly again.

— Well you don't want to go back, do you?

130

I sat up with the blood alive in my veins at the idea and had taken the breath to say *but yes, yes I do*, when he continued.

— To London, I mean.

I shook my head.

— No.

It was the closest we came to discussing what had happened in the monastery. In the silence we heard a sharp stuttering sound in the ceiling as if someone had dropped a ball-bearing that was bouncing across the marble floor in the room above. Rennie got out of bed and began pulling on his socks.

— Sounds like they dropped the microphone.

He laughed and spoke up to the ceiling so that I could watch his adam's apple move up and down.

— You can't fool me, you devil.

I watched my husband dress for his run, as I had watched so many times, and could not understand how everything could be the same after having been so different. I lay with my hands behind my head staring at a knob sticking out of the wall that might have been a pipe, or the head of a badly walled-up corpse. Even after Rennie left the room and went down into the streets — *mens sana in corpore sano* — I continued to lie on the bed and wonder if things could ever be wrenched into some new and better pattern.

18

When we left the *Pensione Dora* in the morning to explore the city, Rennie spotted the sign in the next street: *Pensione Piccadilly*.

— Look darling, he said. I bet a couple of Brits run it.

He held me round the waist and stared up at the sign.

— Let's go in and ask.

I could see that my husband was hungry now for English conversation that could be relied on to mean what it seemed to, perhaps a discussion of cricket scores with some red-faced expatriate who'd settled here after the war. However, the man behind the desk in the gloomy lobby, where everything was made of streaked pink marble like meat, did not look English, and when Rennie spoke to him he began to smile and move his hands around nervously.

— Must be this fellow's boss we want, Rennie told me. He smiled at the man and asked:

— *Padrone? Dov'è il padrone?*

The man kept smiling but shook his head helplessly until his whole face opened in a sudden gape of comprehension. He began pounding himself on the chest.

— *Io sono il padrone. Io, io.*

Rennie stared blankly. I tried to help.

— *Parliamo italiano?*

I had asked this several times, seeing the man smile in bewilderment, when I realized that I was not asking what I meant to.

Rennie glanced from me to the *padrone*, who was

132

prostrating himself so humbly over the marble counter that he was almost lying on it. Frowning in concentration, Rennie spoke with a clarity reserved for the deaf or imbeciles.

— *Parla inglese?*

The man collapsed behind the counter with a look of terrible consternation.

— *Mi scusi, mi scusi. Non parlo inglese.*

— He doesn't speak English, Rennie told me.

It took fifteen minutes of interrogative grunts, much large gesturing, and every word of our combined Italian, to discover that there were no English people in charge of this *pensione*, just Fabbio, but that there were rooms vacant.

We disappointed the fat lady, Dora perhaps, at the *Pensione Dora*, when we told her we planned to move to another *pensione*. She rubbed her hands together and asked which one we were going to and Rennie answered quickly:

— Oh, forgotten the name. He glanced at me, saying, You can't remember either, can you darling?

Our first night in the *Pensione Piccadilly*, I was the one unable to sleep. I lay stiffly next to Rennie listening until my ears seemed about to burst, for footsteps in the corridor, and imagined, or planned, what I would have to do. My shoes were under the bed, my clothes on the chair, and the suitcase was still packed and ready to go. I would have to get my toothbrush and comb out of Rennie's bag and not forget to collect my passport from Fabbio. I heard only the blood pounding in my ears and Rennie's regular breathing as the square of window slowly became lighter with the dawn seeping into the room. Here on the second floor it would have been impossible for anyone to tap on the window and beckon me out, and the drainpipe was almost certainly not strong enough to support even a light body trying to climb up or down it.

It was difficult to explain to Fabbio about *Necessary Catastrophe* and so on, but each afternoon now, I set up the typewriter at one of the tables in the chilly dining room, watched by a dozen sticky bottles of oil and vinegar and sometimes, through a crack in the kitchen door, by Fabbio. Each afternoon on the stroke of four o'clock, he brought me a cup of opaque black coffee, placing it without speaking on the table beside the typewriter. When I thanked him he seemed panicked at so much sound, and glanced around like a conspirator with a hand over his mouth. Among the cloying smells of hundreds of old breakfasts and dinners, I began to type the last chapter, while upstairs Rennie sat making final revisions at the chest of drawers in our room, his bottle of water beside him and wax plugs in his ears.

Don't know why I never thought of them before, he told me, and wore the earplugs more and more often. I found they were so effective that I could carry on long conversations with myself or with a companion of my own invention, while he lay next to me reading. I only had to make sure that I could change a word into a cough or a yawn if he happened to glance at me or if my companion was funny enough to make me laugh. In the mornings I had to shake him awake—if left alone, he might have slept for ever in the silence of the wax plugs— and we got up early, so as to be out in the city before the sun was too hot.

At breakfast we planned our morning. Rennie had never before shown much interest in art galleries, churches, or palaces, but in Milan he had become an indefatigable tourist and seemed determined to view every edifice mentioned in the guidebook. We had inspected the interior of the *Duomo* at length, had consulted the book on the significance of the mosaics in the *Galeria*,

134

and had discovered that *La Scala* was closed for the month. The only major tourist attraction that Rennie seemed to have no interest in was the fresco of *The Last Supper*.

— Wonderful place, this, Rennie said. Florence and all that was pretty overrated, I thought.

In fact, I was beginning to find Milan dull, but Rennie continued to enjoy the swaying trams, the labyrinthine cobbled streets of the centre of town, and the elegance everywhere, as much as if he had discovered it all himself. *Never seen so many well-dressed women*, he remarked daily. *Look at that one, darling*.

He bought a smart pair of sandals for himself from a wizened man in a stuffy shop, and a ruffled blouse for me that I felt obliged to wear now and then rather than the simple shirts I preferred. *Lovely, darling*, he said. *You're so pretty in something a bit dainty*. He stopped to stare into the window of every jewellery shop we passed, and always pointed out the rings that were most heavily ornamented. *That would be pretty on you, darling*.

Soon after our arrival in Milan, he decided that his hair was much too long. He pulled irritably at where it was beginning to curl down his neck, and would have cut it himself, but we discovered that, in the haste of leaving San Giorgio, we had left the scissors behind. He and I sat in adjacent chairs at the hairdresser's and he kept making scissoring motions until the stylist had given him the sleek short fur of a well-groomed dog.

— Would you recognize me, darling? he asked, and was pleased when I assured him that I would not.

I was not sure what I wanted for my own hair, and communicated by gestures to the stylist until my reflection satisfied me. I had never worn my hair so short or so boldly cut, but found my reflection in some way reassuring when the haircut was finished, although Rennie wondered, frowning, whether it was not *a bit severe, darling*, and it was necessary to remind him that it would soon grow out.

Not far from the *Pensione Piccadilly*, coloured neon strips announced a *Palazzo di Tango*, and each time we passed it Rennie squeezed my hand. I knew it was only a matter of time before he would suggest a night of dancing. *And you can wear your pretty new blouse,* he would say.

Between sightseeing in the mornings and working on *Necessary Catastrophe* in the afternoons, we always went up to our room for a short siesta. Once by mistake Rennie had called it *our fiesta* and was careful now to repeat the mistake every time he used the word. He stripped down to his underpants and while I watched from the bed he did an energetic series of exercises. Those first days in Milan, he had put on his running shorts and gone out in the streets for a jog. But both times he had returned quickly and pretended not to hear when I asked him if anything was wrong. Now he exercised in the privacy of our room and afterwards lay on the bed beside me, holding two small knobs of wax and kneading them until they softened.

— Any last words?

I smiled and shook my head. After he had squeezed the wax plugs into his ears it did not take long for his face to take on a blind vacant look and for his breathing to become as regular as if he was doing yoga. Then I lay and watched the spidery man on the ceiling and listened to the people in the next room. Each day as I stared up at the fine cracks in the ceiling I could see more. Now I could trace a pair of straggling legs with long feet, and a spindly arm that sprouted from one shoulder. He was cut off at the neck by the wall, but I thought I could make

136

out a wavery line appearing faintly between his legs, and had a feeling that it was growing a little longer each day. I had not pointed out the ceiling man to Rennie, and had never told him what happened in the next room. Sealed behind his earplugs, he slept through it all.

The shouting began gradually but the voices soon roared and shrilled. Once, crouching against the wall with Rennie's water-glass against the plaster, I caught a few words — it sounded like *watchband*, and then *Grapes! Grapes!* Although the glass increased the volume, the wall had a distorting effect on the words. When the collapsing crashes began, as if bookcases were being spilled onto the floor, the shouting stopped. In the pause that followed the last crash, something hit the wall and fell with a metallic tinkle. It sounded like the same thing every day, but on some days I decided it was a garter belt, and on others I thought it must be a length of chain.

A corner of sheet filled like a tiny sail with each breath Rennie puffed out as he continued to sleep. Still on the floor beside the wall, I squirmed out of my jeans and felt the marble cold on my buttocks. I could hear wheezing from the next room, as though someone was squeezing the air out of flabby balloons. By the time I heard the regular tapping of our neighbours' bed-head against the wall, my hand was moving quickly and I was breathing hard as if climbing a hill. I reached the top of the hill and swooped down the other side at the same moment that the tapping became louder and then stopped abruptly. I had always wanted to be part of a *ménage à trois*.

19

It would have been simple to find out for certain which couple was staying in the next room, but I preferred to glance around and try to guess each morning when the breakfasts were being brought, while Rennie folded down interesting pages in the guidebook. The only other couple who had stayed longer than a night or two sat at the next table. The man abstractedly massaged his bald scalp with his fingertips while his grey-haired wife folded her napkin in four and ran it between the tines of her fork. When she met my glance she smiled comfortably and began to wipe the napkin round and round her plate. I looked away but knew that she would have wiped everything in front of her by the time breakfast arrived. On those mornings when anguished Italian could be heard from the kitchen, as though someone in there was sawing at their wrists with a blunt knife, the woman had time to wipe all her husband's tableware as well while he palpated every inch of his skull. I had never heard either of them speak except to say a very loud *Thank you* to Fabbio when he brought the breakfast.

The two English sisters who blushed so easily had also been at the *Piccadilly* for some time. Rennie had translated for them once or twice at breakfast — *più burro*, he had said loudly, pointing at the girls' plates and making wiping motions with an imaginary knife – and now they both smiled and blushed warmly at the table-cloth when he came in with me, and sometimes whispered *hello* to him across the room.

In the kitchen something dropped with a crash and there was a short scream. Rennie glanced up and held himself tightly, as if waiting for the shots. When he met my eye he said quickly:

— I've just been thinking. What about that market today? You said you wanted a hat.

He nodded, as if a problem had been solved.

— And then tomorrow the roof of the *Duomo*.

We asked Fabbio about hats.

— *Cappello*, Rennie enunciated ringingly, and left a large damp thumb-print on the page of the phrase-book.

Fabbio came out from behind the counter wearing a striped pyjama-top under his jacket, beaming as he approached Rennie. He kept dancing forward like a fencer until Rennie, thumbing helplessly through the phrase-book, had backed into me away from the torrent of Fabbio's Italian. Fabbio darted forward as if going in for the kill, snatched the book out of Rennie's hands, flipped through it, and jabbed at the word in the dictionary section at the end.

Rennie peered closely. *Aspettare*, he read aloud. *To wait.*

Fabbio held up his palms like the Pope blessing a crowd and kept saying *to wait, to wait*. Each time his pronunciation distorted the words a little more so that he was saying *duada, duada*, by the time he disappeared backwards into his room off the lobby. He returned at a trot with an armload of different hats, and slapped each one on his head, posed for a moment, then whipped it off. Under a wide straw hat with spotted feathers in the band he looked like a bankrupt peasant, while under the furry winter cap he was like a thug from the Kremlin. For no reason I thought of Viola. I thought I heard someone say my name and turned quickly, but it was only the English sisters fluttering their fingers and whispering *bye bye* as they set off for a day in the art gallery.

With laborious care, as if he had only just learned to hold a pencil, Fabbio wrote *PP* on a piece of paper and jabbed at the letters, showing them to Rennie, until they were freckled with dots. He began to draw a map to show the way to the market, but started too close to the bottom of the page. He crumpled the paper up and snatched at another from under the desk, crying *Aspetti, aspetti!* On the second sheet he started too near the edge and made tiny moaning noises as he tried to cram the sheets together. Finally he whipped the page over like a magician and finished on the other side. The word *Mercato*, where the map ended, started small but the last three letters were gigantic.

I had become so used to the hissing and sucking noises in the streets that I no longer heard them. Rennie had never heard them before we came to Milan — *Just your imagination, darling,* he had always said, *and anyway it's a compliment.* Now he heard them everywhere. Several times, as we followed Fabbio's map to the market, he stopped dead in the middle of the pavement and turned to stare back at the man we had just passed. I prepared myself to restrain him physically if he started to go after someone with his fists up. *Just thought I saw someone I know,* he would say when I asked him why he had stopped, or, *Just remembered something I'd forgotten.* We had to pass so close to three men lounging at the entrance to the market that I could see how the lips of one had cracked so that they bled, and how a tiny gold ring gleamed in the hair that curled out of another's ear. Rennie took long strides past them and gripped my hand until I felt the bones might crack.

In the market, the crowds were so thick among the stalls and twisted trees that it was impossible to move at a normal walking pace. Rennie and I shuffled along with the crowd while stall-owners leaned on their counters and watched everyone. Two fruitsellers attracted custom by tossing their wares over the heads of the crowd, and it did not seem accidental when a peach landed neatly at Rennie's feet and spattered on the stones. I looked up in time to catch a falling plum but when I wiped it on my shirt and bit into it I found it unripe and bitter. A fat young man with flabby pectorals quivering like breasts under his shirt came up against Rennie in the crowd and they both stepped sideways at the same moment to make way. The man's chin wobbled as he shook his head and grinned, showing a pair of deep dimples, each time he and Rennie met head-on again. Rennie was panting and smiling and making small fan-like gestures with his hands. Finally both men took a step forward at the same moment, collided, and staggered for a moment in a tottering embrace. The fat man slapped Rennie on the back and laughed, calling out *Caro, caro mio* so that people turned to look, and Rennie was wiping his palms on the seat of his jeans when he caught up with me again. He whirled around when there was a catcall from somewhere in the crowd as though it was meant for him.

—Nothing, nothing, he said when I asked him what the matter was. Nothing.

He moved out of the current of the crowd into a backwater of clothing stalls and tweaked at a cheap bright dress hanging up.

—Let's buy you one of these, darling, it'd suit you.

He took the dress down and held it against me, trying at the same time to stand back to see the whole effect. A woman in an identical dress bloomed out from behind the counter, bearing her huge breasts in front of her like a figurehead.

—*Prego, prego.*

Her smile was speckled with gold. Taking the dress

from Rennie, she hung it over my shoulder and prodded me behind a curtain that hung from a tree.

—*Bella, sì, sì.*

Her breasts shook as she closed the curtain with a dramatic flourish, enclosing me so snugly that there was no room to turn around. The bottom of the flimsy curtain did not reach down even as far as my knees, and the top sagged on its string below the level of my shoulders. Standing looking out, feeling the fabric of the curtain gritty against my skin, I met the gaze of several women inspecting large pink underpants at the next stall, and decided not to bother trying on the dress. Over the top of the curtain I could see that Rennie was enjoying a lively conversation, holding up one of the dresses and pointing at its bodice, then gesturing with both hands like a fisherman describing the one that got away.

—*Grande*, he said loudly and nodded at the stall-owner. *Lei, piccola.*

She understood immediately.

—*Ah sì! Sono grossa*, she said, elongating the word like an opera singer and running her hands down in front of her bosom.

—*Lei, piccola.*

She jerked her thumb towards where I stood behind the curtain, then snatched the dress from Rennie to demonstrate how the bodice stretched to fit all sizes. Grinning into his face and pressing her breasts together with both hands, she presented him with a deep freckled cleavage and said in English:

—You see? You see now?

I looked away and met the eye of an old man with a bald dog on a leash, who raised his hat and winked elaborately at me. Turning my back and facing into the bark of the trunk, I watched an ant struggle in a crack, and the scar where the tree had grown a black lip around a piece of metal. This sneering mouth must have been working patiently for years to engulf the metal, and would finally succeed in swallowing it as if it had never existed. I wondered whether a human body strapped to the bark of a tree would eventually be hidden in the same way.

When I stepped out from behind the curtain, Rennie was leaning against the counter laughing at something the stall-owner had said.

—No good. Just didn't look right, I said, tossing the dress on the counter and shrugging at the woman. Rennie seemed reluctant to leave.

—Looks good on her, he said, and for a moment we both stared at where the woman's breasts strained at the fabric. As she reached up to show us another kind of dress and revealed a bearded armpit, I led Rennie away.

Finding the straw section of the market was more difficult than Fabbio had promised. Several times we found we had wandered in a circle and were in the butchers' section again, where chunks of bright red meat lay on stained wooden blocks and the air smelled of blood. The third time we stood looking at lumpy sausages and purple-stamped carcasses, Rennie dropped my hand and strode across to where a woman was pointing out the exact salami she wanted. I could not hear their conversation, but saw the woman look suspicious as Rennie said something and pointed to her hat. He came back smiling and took my hand with authority.

—This way.

We were standing fingering hats at one of the straw stalls when a man's head and shoulders slid silently out from between the mats hanging in front of the counter. His grin at us exposed two missing front teeth, and canines that seemed over-long, as though they had grown down further in compensation. He grinned at me, then at Rennie, displaying his gums with pride.

—Buon giorno, amici!

His words came out in a sibilant hiss that reminded me of Domenico and the daily conversation about the bread. The only difference for him now was that he would collect one loaf of bread instead of two from the village each day. *Come back any time*, Viola had said. Once in Florence, I was sure I could find my way to San Giorgio, although I would not know quite how to address a letter.

The stall-owner leaned further towards us like someone with a rude secret to whisper and three straw mats slithered down together with a liquid sound. Rennie leapt back as if bitten and the stall-owner snickered behind his hand. His loose shirt made his arms twig-like, and was covered with a pattern of female lips and the word *BACI*. Slipping out from behind his counter, he picked up one of the mats that lay like an empty skin at his feet and shook the dust off it so hard that it snapped in the air.

— Vairy good, vairy cheap.

He forced the corner of the mat into Rennie's hand, closing the passive fingers around it.

— Super quality!

He was as indignant as if someone had contradicted him. Pressing closer to Rennie, he pointed to the decoration along the mat's edge, the secrets hidden in the weaving. Rennie backed away and dropped the corner of mat.

— We wanted a hat, actually. Or two, rather, he corrected himself with a gusty laugh.

The man coiled down under the counter and uncoiled a moment later on the other side, holding a mirror. Reaching up so that the sleeve of his shirt fell back and exposed tattoos covering his biceps, he unhooked a floppy hat like a broken paper bag and pushed it onto my head. Rennie stared doubtfully, but the stall-owner cried:

— *Oh sì, bella, bella!*

Drawing Rennie close to him with a hand on his arm, he muttered out of the side of his mouth as if the two of them were thinking about buying me.

— You like, huh?

His gums, where the front teeth had been, were the grey of chewed gristle.

— You husband? he asked suddenly and gave Rennie a poke in the chest that made him step backwards. Husband?

I had to remind myself that anyone would seem to be leering if they had no front teeth. The man had found a hat of pale straw that he pulled over Rennie's head, but immediately snatched if off again and began squashing it between his hands like an accordion to demonstrate how it sprang back into shape when released.

— For the voyage. For the travel.

Crushing the hat flat on the counter, he mimed a suitcase being closed on it, then rolled it up into a tight tube of straw and flourished it in Rennie's face.

— Raffia, is raffia, no straw. Bend, see. Bend and make like little, see?

Rennie's tolerant smile suddenly changed to an expression of great fear as the man seized him by the hips and began fumbling with his pants. Rennie grunted and strained to pull away, but the man kept him in his embrace until he had thrust the rolled-up hat into Rennie's pocket.

— Raffia, see, okay.

Rennie grabbed at the hat sticking up from his pocket and jerked it out. In his hand the hat unrolled and opened up like something alive and the man crowed in triumph.

— Very cheap.

Holding up both hands, he opened and closed the fingers in quick mouth-like gestures, signalling the price. Rennie tried to back away but stumbled over a nest of baskets behind him. He stood paralysed then, holding the

145

hat in both hands ready to rip it apart, his eyes wide, one foot jammed in a basket. Although his face was white, his ears were violently flushed.

— Looks good, I said. Might as well buy it.

I watched the stall-owner smoothing Rennie's money on the counter, caressing the shabby notes, wrinkled as skin. I could remember now where it was that I had recently seen a hat like this one. The stall-owner's tongue flicked in and out between his lips as he concentrated on rolling the hat into a tight tube to present to Rennie. I was finding it hard to keep looking at those exposed lumpy gums.

— *Ciao*, Rennie said loudly, grabbing my hand, kicking the baskets out of the way, and shouldering through the crowds away from the stall. Only when we turned a corner and found ourselves in the nut section did he slow to the shuffling pace of the rest of the crowd.

— Like Dracula with those teeth, wasn't he?

He shuddered.

— Good hat, though.

Letting it unroll in his hand, he twirled it on a finger.

— Handy, really, being able to roll it up like that.

I watched a woman plunge her hands deep into a barrel of glossy hazelnuts, relishing their cool slippery shells.

— It's very nice, I said. Daniel has one just like it.

I wondered why I had used Daniel's name when what I was thinking of was the way the hair branched all over Hugo's body and the way his eyes were invisible under his hat. Rennie stumbled on a cobblestone.

— I never saw it, he said accusingly.

Thinking of that breathless clearing filled with the monotonous whistling of a bird, I said:

— I only saw it once.

Rennie flattened the hat between his hands and crammed it into his pocket, where it bulged oddly. He led the way in silence, gripping my hand so tightly that an unpleasant suction was formed between our damp palms. Finally I thought to stop and buy a bag of almonds.

—Good idea darling, Rennie said, and let go of my hand at last, walking along cracking the nuts loudly with his teeth. He filled his pockets with the shells, waiting to empty them on our return to the *pensione*, but I dropped mine on the pavement as we walked so that there was an unmistakable trail behind me, through all the streets we had walked down. Anyone who had cared to would have been able to follow me.

20

Fabbio had taken on Malthus as a personal *amico*, and when the afternoon came on which I could say *il libro è finito*, he cried out with joy. He darted out of the dining room, where I sat with the last page of Rennie's notes, the one with *The End* written in red at the bottom, and came back with oozing pastries and a bottle of Amaretto. He thumbed admiringly through the pile of typescript while I tried to explain about the carbon copies and the possibilities of fire and flood. When Rennie came down, flushed with completion, Fabbio shook hands with him at length, and then with me, and we all raised our little glasses.

— To catastrophe, Rennie said, and Fabbio repeated:
— *Dacatastrofo*.

Everyone agreed it was time to celebrate.

That night we went dancing and Rennie wore the spotted bow tie that made me think of seals balancing balls on their noses. He steered me towards the lights at the end of the street, which now spelt out *Palazzo di ang*. Every shopfront was shuttered and barred, fastened with heavy brass padlocks, and the pavements were piled with rubbish. A low black streak shot across in front of us and I stopped, feeling my arm tugged by Rennie's as he kept walking.

— Cat, he said.
— No, rat.

I spoke sideways and he did not hear me.
— Mother would say it's bad luck, he said, and his teeth glittered.

—It was a rat.

I gathered up my long skirt in one hand and felt the heel of my shoe sink into something soft.

—Hang on, shit I think.

Rennie turned and waited, silhouetted by the neon so that there was a nimbus of tweed-fuzz around his shoulders. Fabbio had told us that the patrons of the *Palazzo* wore their best, and although Rennie looked hot, the tweed was his only jacket. He took a step closer to me as I scraped something off the sole of my shoe, and at that moment part of the darkness of a doorway swayed towards me with outstretched hand. A long shred of tattered cuff dangled in the light and a button glittered wetly. There was a hoarse sound and I caught a glimpse of a streaming open mouth with no teeth. The man stood with cupped palm, unmoving as I passed close by him. I imagined how his nostrils must be full of my scent.

—Come on, Rennie muttered, taking a step towards me that made his metal-tipped heels strike the pavement sharply. There was a tearing hawk and spit behind us and I gathered my shawl more tightly around my shoulders even though I could feel my back damp with sweat. At the entrance to the dance-hall, Rennie smoothed the lapels of his jacket with a glance at me.

—Your shoe, he hissed. Is it okay?

Balancing myself against a railing that crumbled into rust under my hand, I pulled my shoe off to sniff at it while Rennie glanced uneasily up and down the street.

—Ready? he asked before I had had time to rebuckle my shoe. He was impatient as he hurried me up the steps with a hand under my elbow, as if we were about to be caught red-handed at something.

In the dimly-lit ballroom, Rennie and I found a table near the dance-floor and a sweating waiter immediately brought us two glasses of something red. Rennie looked at his in dismay and caught the waiter by the elbow as he was turning to go.

—Vino? he asked, Vino, or Scotch?

The waiter pressed his lips together as if Rennie had made an offensive suggestion, and turned away. Rennie's hand hesitated over the red drink and he watched as I picked mine up and took a long swallow.

—It's fine, I said. Must come with the door price.

Rennie sipped carefully as if he expected it to bite back.

Red drinks were scattered on all the other tables around the dance-floor, but the unremitting throb of the tango made conversation difficult. Most of the noise came from a fat man playing an accordian, perched high on a stool and wearing lederhosen. Many women had come here alone or in small groups and they twirled their drinks and puckered their lips towards the straw while they glanced covertly at the men who stood around the walls or sauntered up and down between the tables. At the next table, four bare-shouldered and overweight girls sat giggling. One of them had dislodged a false eyelash and was trying to re-attach it, but it stuck each time at an erratic angle that made her look as if she had had a stroke.

—Look at them, Rennie said, undoing the buttons of his jacket. They're going to wet themselves.

He seemed startled to hear himself say this, and looked sharply at me and coughed. The girls' plump shoulders shook as they all tittered together and glanced around and in the dim light, the lipstick on their mouths looked almost black and there were deep shadows between their breasts.

—Of course they go to fat pretty quickly.

Rennie took a large mouthful of his drink and rinsed it around his teeth before swallowing loudly. At another table nearby, three old women sat in silence, all shining in satin and brocade. One fingered the row of spit-curls hanging over her forehead and another patted the tiara that was perched on her frizzed hair. A charm bracelet glittered as the third woman stroked her throat with the gesture of a man checking his shave. She sat monumental in her gleaming satin and her wrists, thick with muscle, defended her red drink. One forefinger tapped the table in time to the music and was the only part of her body that moved. In the shadows, men in dark suits smoothed brilliantined hair with the palm of a hand. One of them approached and whispered something that made the muscular woman snicker before she rose with him to dance. Her companions stared after them expressionlessly.

—Those women look like madams, I whispered.

The woman with the tiara glanced sharply towards us and I had to remind myself she was too far away to have heard.

—Like who?

Rennie cupped an ear with a hand and read my mouth.

—Like madams, I hissed.

He stared at me and I wondered if I'd have to explain what a madam was.

—Oh. I see. Yes I suppose they do.

He shifted his chair away from me, putting an end to our conversation. As he watched the dancers his profile was expressionless.

The band leader, a short sweating man in a yellow tuxedo, leaned towards the microphone and spoke at length while the accordionist slid off his stool and pulled his lederhosen down from where it was wedged in his crotch. The band leader's voice boomed and crackled hugely and was so distorted it could have been English he was speaking. I seemed to hear a phrase or two very clearly: *socks in the loom*, he said, or was it *soul-searching room?* When he stepped away from the microphone he waved his arms like someone guiding an aircraft and the band struck up another tango.

—This red stuff's pretty deadly.

Rennie was standing beside the table.

—You be okay here for a minute?

I nodded, but as soon as the door marked *signori* had swung closed behind him, I found that a tall man in a soiled white suit had sat down beside me. He spoke to me with great charm and showed small even teeth as he smiled. He was inviting me to dance and I found that I was flirting and simpering as I protested.

—*Ma sono inglese*.

The man shrugged his padded white shoulders and took hold of my fingers.

—*Non parlo italiano*, I said.

He brought my hand to his mouth, although I did not feel his lips on my skin.

—Dansa, he said. No talka.

I had already stood up when I remembered to try to explain that I didn't know how to dance, but I had not found the words before we were on the dance floor and I was feeling his erection against my thigh. One hand in the small of my back pressed me close to him but the other held my arm out rigidly like someone demonstrating lifesaving so that I shuffled uneasily between his feet. I had learnt a few steps at school, where the leathery gym-mistress in her running shorts had barked at us—*one, two, cha-cha-cha* — but had lost interest after a few lessons.

I tried to keep the table in sight so that I could see when Rennie came back, but the white suit propelled me forcefully around to the other side of the room. As he had promised, he made no attempt at conversation, but worked at pressing as much of his lower body as he could against mine. Over his shoulder, I suddenly saw Viola reflected in one of the wall-mirrors and was about to call out above the music and free myself from my partner, when I realized that it was not Viola, but myself in my new haircut. I was thinking about the way Viola's smile lit her face when Rennie's voice startled me.

—Okay darling? You okay with him?

Rennie's flush was visible even in the dim light and he was dancing expertly with two of the overweight girls who had been giggling over the eyelash. He had an arm around the fleshy bare shoulders on each side of him and the three of them were undulating together as though they'd been practising for days. Rennie's school had done its duty by its lads and had paired off the slim-hipped boys with the broad-shouldered ones and taught them all to dance. In the album, I had seen the photograph of Rennie leading his mother around a very shiny ballroom floor somewhere. In spite of his size, he moved very deftly now, even with a woman on either side. I stumbled against my partner's feet and said *sorry*, but he did not seem to be aware of me. I could not be sure whether his eyes were closed or whether he was looking down into my cleavage.

—Yes darling, I'm fine, I called, but Rennie and his girls had swept on and I saw him laughing down at them, not hearing me.

When he joined me at the table at the end of the next dance he was out of breath and the bow tie hung askew from its clip. My partner had said nothing when the dance ended, but had left me on the dance-floor while he walked quickly between the tables to the door marked *Signori*. I had noticed that he was slightly bow-legged, and felt all the women in satin staring as I made my way back to the table. Rennie sat panting and watching the girls he had been with, who were now dancing with each other and blowing kisses to him as they circled past. He continued to be out of breath long after it might have seemed natural for him to recover, but waved at the girls each time they circled around. I had not noticed before how many pairs of women were dancing together.

The dance-floor was lit only by a revolving mirrored ball that threw dusty shafts of light over skin and patches of serge suits. Sometimes the light would catch a glint of wet teeth as someone smiled. An old woman was spotlit for a moment on the edge of the crowd, one silver shoe raised behind her and her skirt belled out to lift her from the floor. The music stopped for a beat like a gasp and the woman paced forwards and backwards precisely and was ready with her head thrown back in abandon when the tango swirled on again. The music thrust and teased salaciously but the dancers touched only at the fingertips, and at their hips when they pivoted on a turn.

— Passing like hips in the night, Rennie suddenly said, and snorted a laugh. I found that I was also laughing and could not seem to stop. Rennie took my hand but I continued to look away at the dancers.

— Louise.

He was watching, waiting so gravely for my full attention that I felt myself contract in fear. He reached into his pocket solemnly, but at the last moment seemed to lose faith in what he was doing and finally thrust the small velvet-covered box into my hand without ceremony. It fitted neatly into my palm and obviously contained some small item of jewellery. I stared at it as if it was about to turn into a toad.

— Well go on, open it.

Rennie's voice cracked, he cleared his throat, and I felt myself flush hotly. An old woman was dancing past, as wrinkled as a raisin, her face with its clown-daubs of rouge lifted in ecstasy. Rennie watched the box in my hand with great concentration. When I kept holding it, he said:

— If you don't like it we can change it.

He frowned.

— Maybe.

I struggled with the box and nearly dropped it before

getting it open. Inside, the round brooch was as dark against the white velvet as a drilled hole.

—Onyx, Rennie said. And look on the back.

I held it up to the light and in one of the shafts from the revolving ball saw that something was engraved there. I held it tensely, waiting for another beam so that I could read it.

—*Felicità* something.

The light had swept on too quickly.

—*Felicità in Italia*, Rennie said. Happiness, or pleasure, in Italy. Like it?

I nodded, and with fingers that were clumsy and numb pinned it to the front of my dress. The weight of the brooch pulled down the fabric so that one nipple was nearly exposed.

—I thought about getting one of those rings, Rennie said. But in the end I thought this was better.

He watched as I drew in my chin, peering down to re-attach the brooch near my shoulder strap. Rennie was restored now, squaring his shoulders around fat women, flirting, confident again that he was a husband. And now that he was restored I began to think again of escape. I was not restored, I was drained and dull, alone with him. I was not beautiful, either, as I sat over my red drink, feeling my face twisted as I strained to see the brooch on my dress. As I sat frumpish and graceless beside Rennie, I could feel the heavy stone dragging at the cloth, slowly tearing loose.

21

After so many red drinks, and so many dances at the *Palazzo*, we both woke up late with dense headaches.

—Where are we, Rennie asked blurrily as he tried to open his eyes. Where are we exactly?

He swung heavily out of bed and went to push open the shutters, and held on to the windowsill, raising and lowering himself on the balls of his feet for his deep-breathing exercises. The air whistled strongly through his nostrils.

—It's Milan, he said at last with satisfaction. And tomorrow we'll go back to London, eh?

He had begun to plan the return to London, and had bought a case of wine, some virgin olive oil, and two cheeses to take back with us. I had been oiling and turning the cheeses every day as Fabbio had shown me, but my mouth became chalky at the idea of having to return to London.

—Come on, Rennie said, standing in the sunlight from the window so that each of his legs was haloed with hairs. Get up darling, today's our last day.

I groaned and buried my face further into the pillow so that even when I felt the bedclothes being pulled down to the foot of the bed I did not have to face the day. When I felt his hand on my buttocks I assumed that it lay there casually while he rubbed his eye or scratched his chin, and by the time I realized that the scratching sound was the jar of vaseline being unscrewed, it seemed too late to resist. *Ah*, Rennie exclaimed in triumph as he thrust further and further into me. *Ah! Ah! Ah! Ah!* I lay and bit deeply into the pillow, whispering into the feathers: *Our last day, the last day.* I became the pillow, the mattress, my husband's engorged organ, anything rather than be myself lying in pain under him, wishing to be elsewhere. *Today*, I promised myself. *Do not be afraid, because today is the day you will leave.*

When we went down to breakfast, Rennie slapped Fabbio on the back and cried *Buon giorno amico mio* so gaily that the few guests still sitting over their breakfasts turned to stare. For once Fabbio did not respond to Rennie's good-humour, but kept shaking his head and frowning. He had not yet shaved and one long hair curled out of each nostril. Rennie and I stood feeling the silence of the dining room press in over the noise of our entry, until Rennie's hand stopped on its way to slap Fabbio's shoulder again. The room seemed very cold when Fabbio finally communicated the fact that the bald-headed Inglese and his wife had been killed in a car crash the day before. Breakfast was brought very promptly and when Fabbio left the room Rennie wrapped his roll in a napkin and slipped it into his pocket.

— Can't eat now, he said. It's awful.

I stopped playing with my own breakfast. I was queasy, and did not want to think about anything at all.

We had to reassure Fabbio that it was not because of his guests being killed that we were leaving, and Rennie went to a great deal of trouble, flipping backwards and forwards through the phrase-book, to praise the beauty of the room, the excellence of the service, and the deliciousness of the food. Finally he promised to recommend the *Pensione Piccadilly* to all his friends in London, and Fabbio smiled at last.

While we were standing in the tomb-like marble dimness of the lobby, the blushing English sisters

157

overheard that we were leaving and came over to say goodbye, their brilliantly white tennis shoes making lascivious noises against the floor. They whispered regrets and good wishes and each sister shook Rennie's hand several times. They ducked their heads orientally at me and I thought I heard one of them ask me *Is he heavy?* but they laughed at something Rennie said just then and I was not sure what I had heard. Now I would never know who it had been in the room next to ours, whether it was the dead Inglese and his wife or these whispering girls, who threw things at each other every afternoon before they made the bed tremble with their passion. We set out in the glare of our last day in Milan, and I was afraid of what I had to do, but full of trembling joy as well.

22

In the square in front of the cathedral, the pigeons flapped a few feet into the air when the bells started to clang. After a moment they dropped back down to the pavement and stalked jerkily from crumb to crumb.

Sauntering couples stopped with their arms around each other and stared up at where the bells swung ponderously in their towers, and the man selling bags of crumbs shuffled against the tide of birds around his feet towards the front of the cathedral. Two men in dark suits emerged together, each walking one half of the carved doors back until they were fully open. From the darkness of the doorway organ music piped reedily out into the square and by the time the bride and groom appeared on the top of the steps, a small crowd of onlookers was staring and smiling.

The bride was almost buried under her masses of lace and flowers and leaned on the groom's arm for support. The two of them stood side by side while the rest of the wedding party jockeyed for position on the steps. One aunt or cousin teetered on the very end of a step but would not retreat to a more stable position. When the photographer made squeezing gestures with his arms, the group on the steps jostled to pack closer together, and the aunt or cousin overbalanced from her step at the moment the photograph was taken.

The bride and groom smiled and stared at each other as if inspecting one another's teeth. While the photographer changed his lens or wiped it with a yellow cloth, their smiles stiffened and when he finally pressed the button they turned their heads away. For one last shot they put their heads together cheek to cheek and smiled brassily, but at the moment the shutter clicked, the bride glanced at her new husband as if to check that he was still there. Her look of calculation and apprehension was caught forever.

A hot dry wind had sprung up from the cracks of the stones and the bride was trying to hold herself down against it. Her hair stood up in stiff spikes where the wind was teasing at it, and her train snapped around her feet, catching dead leaves in the lace and dragging across the pavement. The groom was shiny-faced with sweat and constantly looked at his watch. When the line of black limousines finally arrived, he put a hand under the bride's elbow to speed her along into the car, where they both slumped back against the seat. The groom tore at his bow tie until his neck was bare, and the aunt or cousin took a shot of the broad black back of the car as it moved off.

— The happy couple.

Rennie laughed and turned away and I could not tell whether he was being ironic. I watched him buy a bag of crumbs from the man whose shoes were white with bird-shit.

— Here, go on.

I felt the crumbs sharp against my palm and threw my handful down quickly, too close to my feet, and had to leap back as the birds pecked greedily at my sandals. Rennie scattered crumbs in a methodical arc all around him and tossed a special handful directly at a sickly bird who was never quick enough.

— Here, go on, he called.

His well-aimed handful landed hard on the bird's back, making it flinch and hop away. The sound of dozens of beaks tapping on stone seemed very loud. The crumb-man moved slowly towards us through the fluttering birds balancing on his shoulders, and I saw how his white hat was still brown in the creases. Rennie took hold of my hand and led me towards the base of one of the towers.

—Did you see? he said. His hat's all covered with it.

At the first turn in the stone steps up around the tower, we stopped and looked over the edge. Already the crumb-man, and the tourists lining up their shots of the *Duomo*, were puny and foreshortened. A child in red yelled and ran through the pigeons until they rose past us in a flock with a noise like applause. I saw that Rennie's hands were gripping the edge of the parapet so hard that the sinews in his wrists stood out.

—I'd forgotten I'm bad with heights, he said.

He turned his back on the square and craned to look up. His freckles stood out so clearly they seemed painted on the pale skin of his face. Far above, the top of the tower appeared to be swinging smoothly down in a long arc to crush us both, but I was not ready to die now, I was at last ready to act. Rennie blinked and looked away, but I stared until I was quite sure that the toppling tower was an illusion created by the clouds racing past. I would not allow any toppling tower to interfere with my plans.

—Not far now, I told Rennie. You'll be okay.

He guffawed and glanced back down the steps.

—Doesn't bother you at all, does it?

He bit his lip between his teeth as he began firmly walking up the next flight, keeping his eyes fixed on his feet.

From the big square below where the pigeons pecked and preened, the facade of the *Duomo* was thick and rough, like an elaborately-iced wedding-cake. The surface was covered with bas-reliefs, stone frills, and empty niches just big enough for a pigeon, but here I could see that some of the wedding-cake effect was the accumulation

161

of bird-shit that capped every knob and spur of stone.

Rennie pointed out the worn smoothness of the feet of a saint who stared eyelessly from his niche beside the steps.

— People kissing it, he explained. The book says disease is his specialty.

Further up there was another niche, but the statue was completely wrapped in black plastic so that not even the feet were visible. Rennie stopped and consulted the guidebook.

— S. Bartolomeo. Maybe he didn't do enough miracles.

As we turned the final corner of the steps, the wind pounced. Rennie took off his hat, rolled it up, and jammed it into his pocket.

— It's okay darling, I won't let you blow off, he said and reached for my hand. His eyes were narrowed against the wind and he flinched at each gust as though afraid of being hit by something more dangerous than air.

At this height the roofs of the city gleamed green in the sunlight and lay under the smog as under water. Someone opened a window in the distance and pushed it back so that the glass caught the sun blazingly for a moment. Somewhere else a sheet was hung out to dry on a roof-top line and stirred like a banner, very white against the mouse-grey buildings.

The roof of the *Duomo* was not flat, but sloped and peaked so that it was impossible to see more than a few yards ahead. From down below we had seen a couple of statues up here, but now we saw that there were dozens of them, invisible from the piazza, gesturing at the sky. Each one stood on top of a tapering stone column and stared off into the distance. Some pointed without conviction at nothing, while others unfurled scrolls or clutched shapeless objects. All were pocked and stained from the weather, their features blunted, their hands crumbling away as they pointed or clutched. Only certain folds of drapery near their feet were still as sharp as the sculptor had intended, while those outstretched arms would eventually melt away like soap under a shower. Rennie stopped and glanced from one statue to another as if he'd spotted them creeping closer.

— Pretty pointless having them up here where no one can see them.

His words were feeble in all this space, his breathy laugh wiped away by the wind. I hoped that the builders had not relied on gravity alone and a little crumbling mortar to keep the saints in place.

In the worst places along the catwalk, where the roof abruptly fell away, a handrail had been provided for the weak-hearted. I hung on hard, feeling my palms sweaty on the metal, but Rennie strode along scorning the handrail until two pigeons suddenly burst out of a niche near his feet and at the same moment a great blast of wind shook everything. When he turned to me and mouthed words that were snatched away by the wind, I saw how naked and bulging his forehead was where the blasts had flattened the hair. I had never noticed before how narrow his temples were, as if he'd been a forceps baby.

— Okay darling? Want to go back?

He was pale with fear. I shook my head, feeling ends of hair sting my lips and eyes. The air was full of boomings and blastings that would cover any noise the falling saints might make if the huge weight of stone came swinging down. Perhaps, after all, the builders had thought that gravity and God's grace would be enough. If you were standing in just the right place it would be a quick death.

When Rennie stopped again, I assumed that he'd decided to go back down, and I prepared my response. *Wait for me at the bottom, darling*, I'd say, *and I'll just glance around some more*. Perhaps we would be unable to find each other later, down in the piazza. But when I reached him he took my wrist and pointed up ahead. Between the outcroppings of decorative stone I could see a boy in a leather jacket and cloth cap, but it took me a moment to believe that he was sitting astride a gargoyle that jutted out over the front of the building. The soles of my feet tingled at the thought of all the empty air under him. He sat as quietly as on a placid horse while his girlfriend, whose very short striped frock rippled around her thighs, lined up a snapshot. He might have been staring at the grains of the stone between his legs, or deciding exactly which spot on the ground below would receive his body. The height was enough that it would take several long seconds for a body to unwind in the air. He would twist over and over himself, arms and legs gesturing in the eloquence of terror, until the slow unfolding against gravity would be interrupted and the body would smash apart on the steps below. The scream would be swept away by the wind and all of us, Rennie and I and the girlfriend, would stand staring at the gargoyle and at a startled pigeon flapping up from below.

The boy was showing pointed white teeth as he pretended to lose his balance while his girlfriend kept taking another step backwards with the camera to her eye. The fall might not be immediate, but would perhaps be a leisurely process of overbalancing just a little too far. The grin would slowly transform itself into a gape of disbelief and end up as the tight-skinned snarl of panic. His hands, flailing at the air, might grab at the stone for a second, making his eyes widen with pathetic hope, but his palms would slip over the powdery stone and in the last second he would stare hungrily into someone's eyes. I hoped it would not be my eyes that he would cling to in that last endless moment.

164

I had pictured the scene so vividly that I was shocked to hear myself yelp as the boy grabbed convulsively at his cloth cap. He was too late, the wind snatched it off, tossed it for a moment high in the air, then let it drop, twirling down towards the square. Everything moved at once. Rennie took a step forward as if to reprimand everyone, I remembered to breathe, and the girlfriend's skirt flapped up and revealed striped underpants. The boy squirmed back in quickly, but once he was behind the parapet he craned over the edge, squinting down as if still needing to establish something.

— Bloody idiot.

Rennie was punching the palm of his hand with the fist of the other.

— Bloody idiots, the both of them.

As the boy kissed the girl her dress fluttered up again. She must have carefully considered what to wear in a windy place, and had chosen a dress of vertical stripes and underpants with horizontal ones.

— I almost caught myself wishing he'd fall, Rennie said. He watched me and moved closer, making a gesture of nudging me in the ribs.

— Didn't you?

After a pause that went on a little too long, I licked my lips, already rough from the wind, and said:

— Would have been a scream.

Rennie showed his teeth in a grin that fattened the pink tongue between his incisors.

— A scream, he repeated. It would have been a scream.

He walked away towards where the boy was leaning over the parapet spitting down long fibrous threads of saliva. He straightened up quickly as Rennie approached, took the girl's hand, and ran across the roof towards the steps. I could hear them clattering down in guilty haste.

Rennie laid both hands as if to anchor himself along

165

the parapet before looking over the edge, and he stared down for so long that I wondered if I would have to come and prise him off like a limpet. In one abrupt movement he swung his legs over and sat on the edge peering down between his knees at the drop beneath. I squeezed my lips together so hard I could feel them go numb. *He just went berserk*, I heard myself telling Mrs Dufrey, twisting her pearls and choking herself while tears ran down the powdered furrows in her cheeks. *Nothing I could do, not a thing*. Rennie's head seemed very large on his shoulders from this angle. His arms would shoot straight up into the air as he jerked himself forward over the edge but since he had his back to me I would not have to see the expression on his face as gravity snatched him down. When he twisted around and waved me over with vigorous arm-movements, I held my breath, moving towards him heavily like someone drugged. I came up beside him cautiously, wondering if he would take me over too when he went. Then I saw that there was a wide ledge not far below, and that the whole facade of the *Duomo* was a series of shallow ornamented terraces like the tiers of a cake.

—Think I was going to jump?

Rennie kicked his heels against the stone so that flakes were dislodged and fell onto the sooty debris of the ledge.

—Did I scare you?

He put an arm awkwardly along my shoulder and we stared at the smudged grey line of the horizon while his watch ticked loudly in my ear. Somewhere through the haze to the south, through all that sunny air hanging over fields and roads, Viola and Hugo and Daniel were gathering now in the humming kitchen for lunch, and tomorrow Rennie and I would be on our way to London, unless I made myself act.

—*La Scala*, Rennie said, pointing. See where we get the tram?

The tram-tracks gleamed dully in the sun. Down at street level it was never possible to see where the tracks turned until the tram had already begun to lurch around the corner, but at this height their routes were as plain as if drawn on a map. Closer beneath the *Duomo*, in the square where the pigeons had crowded around the crumb-man and one or two tourists, a leather jacket and striped frock were leaving a wake behind them through the birds.

—They want his cap, suggested Rennie, and they watched as the tiny figures below pointed and gestured up at where the two *Inglesi* sat on the top tier of the facade. After much clustering and gesticulation, the jacket and frock moved away from the crumb-man and cut another swathe through the pigeons as they crossed the square. The birds closed back immediately over the track they left.

I watched a pigeon strut along the parapet towards us. Its tiny round eye stared at me, and each time it blinked I could see the dusty reptilian skin of its eyelid. It pecked at nothing as it jerked along the stone and kept its eyes fixed on me.

—Awful, close up, aren't they?

Rennie leaned across me and hissed loudly at the bird. It cocked its head up and down, staring at the big face thrust towards it, and Rennie hissed again, so hard that a strand of spittle landed on the stone.

—Go on, he shouted, waving his arm threateningly. Get away, go on.

He was lying across my lap now, clicking his fingers at the bird and flapping his hand. It would be quite easy, I thought, to arch myself suddenly backwards so that he would roll over down onto the ledge below. The momentum might even carry him further. Of course, he was much stronger than I was, but I would have the advantage of surprise.

As if my thought had been flashed on the air in front of him like a slide on a screen, Rennie straightened up. My fingers found the corner of the stone and gripped it hard. I would not be taken by surprise. Rennie began tugging at something in his pocket until he managed to drag out the hat. He flapped this at the bird, which took a few jerky steps backwards—I could hear the blunt scrape of its claws on the stone—before it flew up into the air. Rennie watched as it circled up and then swooped in a series of short arcs down into the piazza. The wind blasted at us again, so hard that my hair streamed out in front of my face. I stared down into the square through a flickering tunnel of hair, feeling my scalp exposed along the back of my head. When Rennie turned my face to his and kissed me, his saliva was cold in my mouth.

—You're shivering, he said. Let's go back down.

He kissed me again, forcing his tongue into my mouth and I could see one enormous staring eye. When it blinked I closed my own.

We would go back down past the saint wrapped in plastic, and the saint with the smooth feet, and I would cross the square and make pigeons scatter away from me. I would do my best to step on one but they would always be too quick for me. I would buy the gaudiest postcard on the rack and a pen marked *Saluti da Milano* and remember that the word for stamp was *francobollo*. Rennie might ask who I was writing to but I would ignore him. My message would be so short it would only fill half the space on the back of the card but the address would include everything I could think of. Back at the *pensione*, I would ask Fabbio whether he thought the bus or the train would be better, and I would pack only the smallest bag, with only the most necessary things. What was really necessary? It was hard to think of anything I needed to take with me into the future.

When Rennie drew his face away from mine a strand of saliva dangled for a moment between our mouths. We both wiped our chins and looked away. Rennie held the raffia hat up so that it fluttered and jerked like something desperate to escape.

—I don't want this.

When he opened his hand, the hat fell for an instant before the wind snatched it up and tossed it out away from the building. We watched as it flew over the square, falling and rising and borne along the wind like a boat, turning and floating as it slipped through the air down towards the pigeons.

—Good fucking riddance.

He turned to me and said it again with relish.

—Fucking good fucking riddance.

He made a funnel of his hands in front of of his mouth and I heard how his voice was distorted, some syllables swept away by the wind and others loud and clear, as he yelled down into the square.

—Go to hell, go to hell, fuck off! Go fuck yourselves!

He stayed like that, hands cupped around his mouth, for a long time after he stopped shouting. He seemed to be waiting for some kind of response from the tiny figures down there, but no one looked up. Only the pigeons applauded his moment of greatness, rising in a great thrumming cloud from the square, beating their wings in thunder at my husband's triumph.

I left Rennie in the square with all the pigeons, as I'd hoped I would be able to do. He was beside me as I walked back to the *Pensione Piccadilly*, beside me as I packed my bag, seized my shoulder as I passed him to leave our room. He shouted, he cried, he begged, he threatened me with his open hand. There was a lot of noise, and he slammed the lid of my suitcase down on my fingers so hard I thought they were broken, but nothing could stop me now. In all this mounting haste, finally I left the postcard behind on the bed. *Dear Viola*, it said, *I am coming back*. There was nothing more I could think of that needed to be said.